DEATH WAS WAITING . . .

Then they saw it: a hazy black shape in the darkening deep of the sea.

The woman and Carter dived for the bottom and the sheltering rocks.

They went a few feet and stopped.

They hovered in the water unable to go any further down.

Held.

Caught and immobilized as if in the grip of a giant hand.

Held by some unseen hand.

A force that slowly drew them toward the black, silent submarine . . .

NICK CARTER IS IT!

"Nick Carter out-Bonds James Bond."
—*Buffalo Evening News*

"Nick Carter is America's #1 espionage agent."
—*Variety*

"Nick Carter is razor-sharp suspense."
—*King Features*

"Nick Carter has attracted an army of addicted readers
. . . the books are fast, have plenty of action and just the
right degree of sex . . . Nick Carter is the American
James Bond, suave, sophisticated, a killer with both the
ladies and the enemy."
—*New York Times*

FROM THE NICK CARTER
KILLMASTER SERIES

NICK CARTER

KILLMASTER

The Samurai Kill

C

CHARTER BOOKS, NEW YORK

Dedicated to the men of the
Secret Services of the
United States of America

THE SAMURAI KILL

A Charter Book/published by arrangement with
The Condé Nast Publications, Inc.

PRINTING HISTORY
Charter edition/July 1986

ISBN: 0-441-57284-7

Charter Books are published by The Berkley Publishing Group,
200 Madison Avenue, New York, New York 10016.
PRINTED IN THE UNITED STATES OF AMERICA

PROLOGUE

A thin red dawn tinged the eastern sky over the remote cove not far from the mouth of the Sepik River on the north coast of New Guinea. Rain forest hung thick over the edges of the deep, narrow cove except where small, rickety piers had been built out into the water. Around the piers the jungle had been cleared for access.

The people stood in the clearings around the piers at the edge of the cove.

Naked, ragged, their black skins smeared with dirt, they stood in silence, staring down into the dark water of the cove. Some of them, the older men with white hair and scarred faces, shook their heads in solemn wonder. The younger ones, men and women, licked their lips and balanced nervously on one foot. And all of them continued to look down at the surface of the cove.

They seemed to stare at the water itself. But it wasn't the water. It was what protruded from the water. Moved in the water. Choked the water.

Moved and grew.

Even as they all silently watched in the darkness before dawn, the vegetation grew before their eyes. Not

1

as fast as a fish jumps or a snake swims, but fast enough for the human eye to see.

It grew and choked the cove, filling it. The plant life was already so thick that one of the old men remarked, "Soon we will be able to walk on the water."

The others who heard him, all Christians now, shivered and crossed themselves.

A tall, white-haired Caucasian appeared behind the old man who had spoken. In khaki trousers, shirt, and bush jacket, all faded almost to white by many years of having been washed on rocks and dried in the sun, he was led by an energetic young black in a similar outfit, the young man's still crisp and new-looking.

"You come see!" the younger man urged as he half dragged the older man to the edge of the cove.

The silent people parted to let the two in khaki go to where the old black man waited for the old white man.

"You look," the old black man said, not in his own tribal language now but in Pisin, the pidgin lingua franca of the new nation. The white man nodded. The Australian station agent who had remained to help the new government after independence had lived here most of his life. Where else would he go?

"What is it?" he said.

"Water like jungle. Can walk on water. Fella no here yesterday. All same here now. One night."

"That's impossible."

"Sure. Fella no possible. All same happen."

The tall old Caucasian stared down at the water. As he watched he saw the thick vegetation growing up through the slowly lightening surface of the narrow cove, growing so fast it seemed to be more animal than vegetable, moving across the water like a million snakes with leaves in their mouths. The whole surface of the cove was alive like a single giant sea monster.

Then came the fish.

Dead fish oozed to the surface of the vegetation-choked cove. Hundreds, thousands were emerging everywhere through the thick plant growth. Dead shellfish were carried on the vegetation, their shells open like the mouths of corpses.

And dead animals.

A cat. Two dogs. The gray bodies of rats and mice.

"Boss!"

The tall old Australian looked to where one old black pointed. A muskrat had come to the cove, slipped into the water, and started to swim through the strange vegetation. It swam out five feet, ten feet, then turned on its back, dead.

"Get everyone away from the cove!" the Australian shouted.

The old men needed no urging.

With the tall Australian at the rear they all hurried away from the cove. Before they vanished into the jungle toward their village, the Australian turned around to stare at the unearthly sight. Then he followed the rest at a trot toward the village and his radio.

Silence fell over the cove as dawn slowly lit the landscape; a silence broken only by a strange sibilant sound: the sound of leaves and thick vines growing rapidly through the water. An endless hiss like the distant pound of surf. Growing and thickening. A mass of vegetation that seemed to lift the surface of the water itself.

Then up through the massive underwater jungle, out of the cove, came ten men in black wet suits.

On the shore, they began to trot inland.

ONE

Nick Carter swam into the dark shadows of the coral cave and flattened himself against the jagged wall. Careful to keep his air hose away from the sharp edges of the reef, he waited in the shadows. Brilliantly colored fish swam through the clear blue water, the paler blue light of the surface far above.

The other swimmer appeared around the coral-encrusted wreck of a World War II American landing craft, moving slowly and cautiously, spear gun ready, eyes searching behind the face mask.

The swimmer passed the dark mouth of the small coral cave.

And whirled to suddenly race toward the opening of the cave, spear gun out in front.

Carter waited until the last second, kicked hard off the reef, and dove under the advancing diver.

He almost made it.

The second swimmer doubled like a snake, caught one foot, and pulled. Carter somersaulted in the water and grabbed his attacker by the waist. They wrestled in the deep water far below the distant surface.

Until the smaller attacker caught Carter's swim trunks and pulled them off.

She grinned around her mouthpiece, then reached up and untied her halter, letting her breasts float free in the blue water in the shadows of the great reef. Carter came to her. They held each other under the far-off pale light of the surface, their eyes alive behind their diving masks.

Carter pointed to the sunlit surface and the shadow of their boat.

She nodded, her eyes flashing through the plexiglass of the mask.

They stared at each other for a moment, desire obvious in their gaze.

The sea suddenly darkened.

Carter looked up.

A giant shadow loomed through the water toward them, a shadow that darkened the bottom of the sea like night, a black cloud between Carter and the woman and the light from above.

The two divers glanced quickly at each other. The woman moved her fingers rapidly in sign language.

"A shark?"

Carter answered the same way: "The biggest shark I've ever seen if it is."

"A whale?"

"Could be," Carter signed through the darkened ocean.

"Maybe we'd better hit the bottom."

Carter nodded.

They sank down to the bottom, crouching against the reef as the long shadow moved closer to pass almost directly above them.

It wasn't a shark or a whale.

"A submarine!" the woman signed.

"Not any submarine I know," Carter answered.

It was small and unlike any submarine either of them had ever seen.

It was half as thick as it was long, with windows along the sides, ponderous and slow-moving, yet not all that slow.

"More like a deep-diving submersible for scientific research," the woman signed.

It did indeed look like the kind of diving submersible used far down at the bottom of the deepest water, yet it was bigger and faster than any diving submersible Carter had ever seen.

"Do you recognize it?" he asked through the shadowy water.

She shook her head. She had never seen anything like it either. Her name was Siobhan O'Neill, Commander Siobhan O'Neill of the Australian Navy, and she knew as much about underwater hardware as anyone on earth.

Against the reef they watched the strange submersible pass slowly over them and on out toward the open Pacific. It moved steadily to the southeast and finally faded from sight in the clear blue water.

Carter pointed to the surface, then said in sign language, "We'd better report."

Siobhan O'Neill nodded.

They started up.

The five men came from the direction of the vanished submersible.

Five men swam toward them in wet suits and masks, spear guns out in front, and—no air tanks!

Carter didn't wait.

Neither did Siobhan O'Neill.

They dove back to the bottom and the shadows of the reef.

"Into the reef!" Carter signed.

They swam into the sharp-edged labyrinth of the coral.

The first spear impaled itself in the coral an inch behind Carter's foot as he plunged into the jagged shadows of the reef.

The second tore paint from Siobhan O'Neill's air tank, the metallic clang echoing through the blue water.

They swam in fast curves and turns deeper into the reef itself. The third spear drew blood from Siobhan

O'Neill's thigh. She was an instant too slow to escape the lead attacker.

"Keep swimming," Carter signed.

He curved around a jagged spur of coral, then threw himself into a somersault as Siobhan swam on past.

The lead attacker raced around the coral spur and saw Carter a split second too late. He fired, but the Killmaster's spear caught him in the throat as he pulled the trigger. The man's arm jerked, and the powerful air-propelled spear flew harmlessly over Carter's head.

Thick blood gushed into the water as the dead attacker went limp and floated slowly, like a broken doll, toward the surface.

The others came behind the dead man among the razor-sharp coral shapes and peaks. Carter turned and swam after Siobhan. The other four were almost on top of him as he came out of the reef into clear water.

Siobhan picked off the first one.

The spear protruded a foot out of his back as he thrashed and screamed soundlessly like a fish on a harpoon.

The remaining three ducked back into the reef for cover.

"The landing barge!" Carter signed.

They swam powerfully toward the shattered shape of the encrusted old World War II craft, gliding through the underwater barriers set up so long ago by the Japanese defenders of the atoll—barrels of concrete, jumbles of old railroad tracks, and rusted masses of barbed wire.

Behind them the three pursuers had regrouped and now reached the barriers. Two stopped in time. The third didn't.

Caught by the barbed wire, he struggled to disentangle himself. Carter shot from inside the old landing craft, spearing the struggling man with a single shot across the distance of crystal-clear water.

The man floated among the rusted rails. One more sacrifice in the ruins of a long-ago war, his blood rose slowly through the blue water.

The last two slipped over the wire and the rusted barriers in a final attack on Carter and Siobhan hidden in the cover of the old landing craft.

Siobhan speared one in the left shoulder.

Carter got the other in the right arm.

The pair of attackers turned and fled, their blood leaving a cloudy trail of red behind them.

Carter looked at Siobhan O'Neill, then signed quickly, "You go up and report in. I'll go after them."

"So you get all the fun? Not on your life, Commander Carter. You report, I chase. Or we chase together. When someone tries to kill me, I want to know who and why."

"How's that wound in your thigh?"

"A scratch. It's already stopped bleeding."

Carter grinned behind his mask, and together they began to swim off after the vanishing figures.

They followed the fleeing shadows and the trail of blood in the water. The chase led them away from the reef in the direction of the deeper water, going down rapidly toward the darker blue depths.

They swam low to the bottom, rising and falling in their swimming with the contours of the dwindling reef. The divers up ahead, who somehow breathed without tanks, never looked back. Carter wondered if they were too scared to care if anyone were following them—or too sure it wouldn't matter if anyone did follow them.

"That submarine?" Carter signed to Siobhan.

"That's my guess," she agreed.

"How much air do you have?"

"Maybe another fifteen minutes," she signed, "but we have to get back, too."

"We can go back on the surface."

Then they saw it faintly in the distance: a hazy black shape in the darkening deep of the sea.

The submarine.

It seemed to be resting silently just above the bottom, just on the edge of a sudden plunge down into the blackness of the vast ocean depths.

Silent and unmoving.

The two escaping divers seemed to swim faster as they approached the looming shape.

"Let's get them!" Carter signed through the darker water.

They swam in fast pursuit of their quarry and closed the gap rapidly.

But all at once their two mysterious attackers seemed to stop swimming and move through the water faster than any swimmers could, like projectiles hurtling toward the steel sides of the submarine. Hatches opened in the submarine, and the two men vanished inside as if sucked up by a great vacuum.

"Dive!" Carter signed quickly, urgently.

Siobhan needed no urging.

The woman and Carter dived for the bottom itself and the sheltering rocks.

They went a few feet and stopped.

They hovered in the water unable to go any farther down.

Held.

Caught and immobilized as if in the grip of a giant hand.

Held by some unseen force.

A force that slowly drew them toward the black, silent submarine.

TWO

Carter struggled to break out of the grip of the unseen force that dragged him slowly through the darker water into the deep ocean. Siobhan signed frantically as she twisted and turned beside him.

"What is it?"

"Some kind of force field that's holding us!"

"That's science fiction!"

"Not now it isn't."

No matter how hard they twisted, turned, and struggled against the force that held them, they couldn't break away. Carter stopped fighting, and just paddled slowly in the dark blue of the deeper water. Siobhan stared at him.

"We can't give up!"

"No," Carter signed. "Come on."

He began to swim straight toward the dark shape of the submarine ahead. Siobhan understood at once and swam after him into the power of whatever was dragging them. Their sudden hard swimming, combined with the pull of the force, moved them rapidly toward the silent submersible with its side windows like blind eyes.

They were less than fifty yards away when they realized they were getting no closer.

No matter how hard they swam they remained fifty yards from the silent submarine with its empty windows.

"It's moving!" Siobhan signed.

Slowly, almost imperceptibly, the submarine had begun to move away from Carter and Siobhan O'Neill. It moved slowly, but faster than they could possibly swim, and the force still held them in its grip, so they were dragged through the water.

They could neither escape nor advance any closer to the submarine. They could only struggle helplessly and look at their watches.

"How much air?" Siobhan signed.

"Ten minutes."

"What do we do?"

"Try to break out, and hope."

"Lovely."

They tried everything: twisted, dived, swam ahead as fast as they could, hurled themselves sideways. They tried resisting the pull together, Carter pulling on Siobhan's waist.

Nothing.

They looked toward the disappearing bottom as the land sloped steeply down into the depths of the ocean. If only they could grab a rock, Carter thought, frustrated, but there was no way they could swim down with the force holding them.

They tried to swim to the rear, away from the beam.

Nothing.

"How long?" Siobhan signed.

"Four minutes."

"Less. We have to get to the surface."

"The force beam has to come from somewhere on that sub. Maybe a spear would carry that far?"

"We might as well try anything."

Carter aimed his spear gun and fired straight at the massive black shape of the submarine that pulled them inexorably ahead.

The spear fell far short, and hung dangling vertically in the pull of the force.

"The head!" Carter signed. "Only the head!"

"The shaft is bamboo!"

"Magnetic! The pull is some kind of magnetic force."

"The tanks!"

"Has to be."

"Can we make the surface?"

"We'll have to. Take in all the air you can."

They breathed slowly, then took one long, deep breath and threw off their air tanks.

They kicked upward as hard as they could, and broke free of the force from the submarine.

The air tanks hung suspended in the water, moving on after the vanishing submarine.

Carter and Siobhan O'Neill swam up and up toward the surface.

Kicked up and up.

Slowly let out precious air.

Up and up and up and. . . .

Carter broke out into the air and gulped deep breaths.

Siobhan came up gasping, swallowing water but breathing.

They breathed. Breathed.

Siobhan smiled. "Nice to breathe real air."

"And we can even talk," Carter said with a laugh.

Siobhan laughed too, and in the bright sunlight and air on the surface of the blue Pacific they hugged each other and laughed and laughed. The long swells of the sea rolled them up and over and down again under the lighter blue of the cloudless sky. A massive, ponderous sea that seemed to roll from the vast depths of the Mariana Trench.

"Well," Siobhan said, "what do you think?"

"I think it's nice to breathe and talk."

"The submarine. Do you think it's part of what we're here for? The missing divers? The small moving 'things' seen deep down outside the reef?"

"That could be, but I'm more concerned with where we spotted it, and where it was coming from. It was pretty close to Kwaj, and coming from the direction of the lagoon."

"Soviet?"

"Why? They've got their surveillance ship off Kwaj all the time. Was it a Soviet-type sub?"

"It wasn't any kind of submersible I've ever seen. Fatter and slower than a combat sub. A lot bigger and faster than any deep-diving submersible."

"No clues as to who built it or where it could have come from?"

"None."

Carter nodded where they stroked slowly in place on the heaving rolls of the ocean, and on the crest of a swell he looked all around.

"Any clues to where we are?" he asked Siobhan.

"About four miles northeast of the atoll by now. If we swim due west, we should hit one of the islands around the lagoon."

"You know where west is?"

"I *am* a naval officer, mate," the Australian said. "What do they teach you in that navy of yours?"

"Just start swimming west."

She laughed, flipped her watch over to reveal a waterproof compass, sighted on the sun, and began swimming. Carter swam beside her through the rolls of the open Pacific toward the Kwajalein atoll where he and Siobhan were based for their investigation of the odd happenings at the supersecret U.S. installation. Kwajalein was where the U.S. Marines had landed so bloodily long ago in World War II, where the U.S. Air Force's Ballistic Missile Office sends its intercontinental ballistic missiles to land on their test firings from Vandenberg Air Force Base five thousand miles away in California, and where the supersecret Strategic Defense Initiative research was being done.

In his disguise as Commander Nelson Carter of United States Naval Intelligence, AXE's superagent N3, the Killmaster, and Siobhan O'Neill of Australian Naval Intelligence, had been sent to Kwajalein because native divers had been going down as they always had from where they had been moved to Ebaye Island in the atoll, but some of them had not been coming up. And some of those who did come up, those who had dived deeper than most, brought back stories of seeing odd, black, cigar-shaped objects moving rapidly through the water near the supersecret atoll base. Moving, and no one knew where to or where from.

"Nelson!"

The great dorsal fin cut through the swelling blue surface no more than fifty feet away.

"Stop," Carter said. "Easy."

"A white?"

"Just float, no motion."

They floated as the fin seemed to make a long, slow, lazy curve around where they were motionless in the middle of the vast expanse of endless water. Carter spoke without moving his lips.

"Spear gun?"

"Not much against a white."

"It's something."

The fin went on, not circling them, but simply swimming in a long curve that moved the shark past them but not away from them. They floated, never taking their eyes from the moving fin.

"It hasn't seen us."

"Not yet."

"They don't see well."

"No."

"I'm glad we didn't wear wet suits. People think it makes us look like seals. Slow seals, easy to catch."

"And they like seals."

"I'm not sure how they find . . . things."

"No."

The school of porpoise appeared from out of the long swells. A large school, swimming and gamboling. Adults and young. The great white would not catch a healthy adult, but there was always hope of an injury or one of the calves wandering too far, overlooked by the adults. The slicing fin left its circle and cruised away in a fast, straight line after the lazily swimming porpoises.

"Breaststroke," Carter said. "For a while."

"As long as we get away from here and closer to shore."

They swam, breaststroking for some time, and then changed to the powerful crawls of experienced distance swimmers. For a long time they saw only the heavy swells as they crested and dropped down into the troughs and crested again. On and up and down and on and over and down and on. Watching always for the fin behind and the land ahead.

The fin did not come, but the land did.

First they glimpsed the far-off sight of palm trees that seemed to grow up out of the blue swells themselves, trees in the sky, and gone, then rising into the sky again. And then they saw the white spray of surf breaking on the reef, then the dark flash of the reef itself. And still the tops of the palms inside the reef beyond the spray.

Then they saw the break in the reef, the opening of a passage through.

"It's Bigej Channel," Siobhan said. "We're a lot farther north than I thought."

"How far?"

"Ten miles at least."

Carter glanced toward the sun that now hung low in the western sky behind the atoll.

"We can't swim that much farther south before it gets dark," Carter decided. "Swim into the atoll. We'll land on the first island."

They swam into the wide channel through the reef and on toward the vast atoll ringed by the low-lying coral islands. Darkness fell abruptly, and Carter pointed toward some palm trees and low greenery close by.

"Let's hit shore there before it's so dark we can't see islands or reefs."

Once on the white sand of the shore, they found their

legs shaking from the long swim and the hours in the water. They sat on the still sun-hot sand without speaking, getting their breath and their strength back.

Then they began to shiver.

The darkness was cold with the sun gone.

They moved close together against the shivering cold. Their bodies touched. Cold and tired and silent with the memory of the shark and the force that had held them helpless far beneath the ocean, they remembered the fear and the closeness of death. And suddenly they wanted each other.

"Nelson?"

"It's okay."

"We could have drowned. We could have been torn apart. We could have never come back. Not ever!"

"It's okay."

"We were almost dead."

"Almost."

"I don't want to be dead."

"No," he said. Carter knew that death had been as close as a white shark's eyes and the unknown force of a submarine dragging them down into the depths of the sea.

He picked Siobhan up and carried her into the shadows beneath the palm trees, behind the heavy green leaves and out of the night wind.

He lay her on the soft sand.

She took off her halter, freeing her breasts in the cool night air. They were high and tight from the cold and the ocean. Carter pressed the hard, cold breasts against his chest until they began to warm and soften. He pressed her breasts and her belly. Her hand pulled off his trunks.

Down on the still warm sand he slipped off her bikini bottom and knelt between her legs. She clawed at his naked back, and he spread her wide and wider and entered in a violent thrust that tore a long cry of need from her throat. A cry of relief. Of life. Of triumph over death.

He thrust into her so deeply he felt as if he were far

down in the dark sea again, under miles of water, enclosed and smothered by her body as he had been by the ocean. His hips moved, thrusting, straining deeper and deeper into her. His back and chest were held in a powerful grip by her arms and legs. Her teeth on his neck, her tongue on his throat, her mouth open with low sounds from far down in the depths of time, sounds from a million years ago.

Cries shattered the silent night of palms and hot sand and softly rolling waves of the sheltered lagoon and the far-off rumble of surf on the reef and the open ocean that reached to the ends of the earth. Timeless . . . endless . . . infinite. . . .

The moon was up in the black sky of stars when Carter turned to look down at her beside him in the sand. A sea wind moved the palms above them.

"We're alive," she said.

"Yes," he said.

"On the whole, I think I prefer that."

"It has certain advantages. But it's even better with something to eat and maybe a bed."

"I don't know, Commander—the sand seemed to do fine for our purposes."

Carter laughed and stood up. "What we could use is a telephone. We've got to report in."

It took some time to find her bikini and his trunks in the dark where they had thrown them. They dressed in what little they had and moved through the thick green growth under the palms. They saw no sign of habitation and came out at the edge of the water again in less than fifty yards. They walked along the edge of the water and returned to where they had started in another fifty or so yards.

"It's just a damned islet," Siobhan muttered.

"Which one?"

"How would I know? There're ninety-three of them in the Kwaj atoll."

"And this is probably the smallest."

Across the water they saw another islet, larger, with

an enormous radar dome like a giant's tennis ball against the dark sky. There was no sign of light.

"It could be Bigej Island," Siobhan said. "Whichever one it is, no one is there at night."

"Let's try the other side."

At the other end of their minuscule dot of land, the lagoon stretched calm in the night as far as they could see.

"We're miles from where anyone lives," Siobhan said.

"You feel like swimming south in the dark?"

"With great whites around? Not to mention reefs and God knows what else?"

"Then it looks like we bed down here."

She smiled. "It's been a good bed so far."

"Very good."

"We might as well try it again."

They did.

And after a long time, covered by palm fronds and other thick leaves, they even slept.

THREE

A brilliant sun shined low through the vegetation like a great blood orange. Nick Carter opened his eyes.

He was alone.

He sat up, scattering palm fronds and sand.

Siobhan was nowhere in sight.

Her diving mask, spear gun, swim fins, and bikini lay on the sand next to where they had slept among the thick undergrowth.

Carter reached for his spear gun and jumped up.

On the far side of the tiny islet something splashed through the water of the lagoon.

Carter moved quickly in a crouch through the thick growth under the palm trees, peering out between parted leaves at the western edge of the tiny islet. He saw nothing.

The surface of the lagoon stretched unbroken in the early morning sunlight.

Then she came up, breaking through the surface in a great surge of white water. Siobhan O'Neill, naked, water streaming from her breasts and hair and thighs, playing and cavorting in the lagoon like a slim white porpoise.

She saw him.

"Nels! Come on in!"

He laughed, put down his spear gun, and stood up. He stripped out of his trunks and plunged into the crystalline water of the shimmering lagoon. Siobhan swam rapidly away from him. He pursued in a long, powerful crawl that ate up the distance, but he gained no ground on the swift Australian.

She swam around the point of the minuscule island, then turned on her back and floated as Carter came up. He kissed her where she floated, and in the cool, clear water they embraced for a long time. When Carter carried her out of the water she buried her face in his shoulder and he placed her down on the exact spot of sand where they had spent the long night under the palm fronds.

Then they made love again.

Slowly this time, in no hurry, the smell of death gone with the warm morning sun. Soft and slow, moving sinuously in the sand. Watching themselves and each other, enjoying, smiling down and up, delaying and moving and shaping the moment in the morning sun that moved as they moved, slowly up over the tops of the palm trees.

Until at last their breathing grew shorter and quicker and it was not possible to delay any longer and he exploded into her and—

A mammoth, thunderous, mountainous pillar of water soared into the air in the center of the great lagoon, echoing across the whole Pacific, water raining down like some massive circular Niagara.

"My God," Siobhan whispered hoarsely when she finally caught her breath. "What the hell was that? I mean, you're good, Nels, but . . ."

With the echo of the massive impact and falling water still reverberating across the lagoon, Carter grinned.

"ICBM coming in from Vandenberg," he said. "Until the 'Star Wars' research, Kwaj was mainly just a big bull's-eye for the air force boys to play with."

"Christ, I'm glad they've got good aim."

"On the button from five thousand miles."

Siobhan got up and began to pull on her bikini. "And speaking of buttons, we'd better get dressed and get back to the general with our report."

"You want to swim, or wait to flag down a chopper when the crew comes to that radome over across the water?"

"We've had enough long-distance swimming for a while, wouldn't you say?"

"That I would say. Okay, let's swim over and wait for the crew at the radome."

They did, and less than half an hour later the helicopter appeared, flying low up along the chain of small islands that surrounded the vast lagoon. The civilians who operated the radar equipment, and the army helicopter pilot, gaped at the two half-naked divers with their fins and spear guns, until Carter and Siobhan O'Neill produced their identification and top-secret ratings from the waterproof pockets inside their bathing suits. The civilians continued to gape and grin, but the pilot snapped to and ushered them aboard the chopper for the trip south to Kwajalein Island itself.

They flew low over the white line of the reef with the massive blue Pacific stretching like a great bowl in all directions, the edges rising at the horizons as if the endless blue would engulf them. Carter watched the reef and the long chain of islets below, big and small, with the pale blue lagoon contained inside, the distant islets out of sight on the far side of the largest atoll in the world. He saw empty islands, and radar domes, and great tracking satellite saucers, and the larger Ebaye Island where all the native Kwajaleinis were packed now in a kind of paradise slum, and finally the larger, elbow-shaped, main Kwajalein Island.

As they hovered waiting for a pad at the headquarters of the army officers who ran the complex, Carter and Siobhan looked down on the mile-square island with its coconut palms, and old Japanese bunkers, and the high-technology community that had sprung up since the

U.S. Army had taken over. The surf-pounded island was home to about three thousand Americans, only thirty of whom were military personnel. The rest were engineers, technicians, and other civilian workers with their spouses and children.

Even from the air, except for the expanse of endless water, palms, and surf, Kwaj could be a small town anywhere in mid-America. There were two nine-hole golf courses and a pair of swimming pools, high school proms and a VFW Post, rock music on the radio and seven brands of beer in the single bar. The only difference, beyond the sweep of the Pacific, was that this town's Bermuda-shorts-clad workers were all experts in radar, optics, missile guidance, and other exotic mathematical disciplines.

They were men and women from MIT, RCA, GTE, and Kentron. They pored over pages of mathematical formulas as they commuted daily to the atoll's far-flung facilities aboard army aircraft. The billion dollars' worth of equipment included the mammoth radar dishes shaped to a hairsbreadth tolerance and pumping out 400 billion watts of power—including the massive, 150-foot-diameter Altair that tracked Soviet satellites with uncanny accuracy, telescopes that could pick up a 17,000 mph missile, 2,000 miles away and hold it in their sights, and high-tech video cameras of incredibly advanced design.

The greatest tribute to Kwaj's one-of-a-kind technological development was the Soviet electronics-surveillance ship that lay constantly just offshore picking up the streams of encoded data being beamed back to the United States, data that included every nuance of how an ICBM, its warheads and decoys, performed, and that recently contained the island's most spectacular accomplishment: the triumphant culmination of the ten-year, $300-million "Homing Overlay Experiment."

An unarmed ICBM was launched from Vandenberg toward Kwajalein. Ten minutes later an anti-ICBM missile was fired off Kwaj. Using a new infrared homing system, the heat-seeking Defender missile caught the ICBM's warhead more than a hundred miles up in space over the Pacific and destroyed it in a collision that flashed explosively across the island's ultrasensitive sensor screens.

But as Carter and Siobhan O'Neill came into a landing, the headquarters island of the whole supersecret complex looked as peaceful as any American town or suburb thousands of miles from any international danger. Only it wasn't, and something was wrong in paradise. Carter and Siobhan hurried into the headquarters of the commanding officer. The master sergeant outside the commandant's office jumped up when he saw them.

"The general's been looking for you two since yesterday afternoon. Come on."

The sergeant knocked, opened the commandant's door, and peered in.

"Carter and the Australian cloak-and-dagger, sir."

A deep, curt voice growled in response, "It's about time, dammit! Send them in."

The sergeant stood aside, winked, and they walked into a large, comfortable office that could have been on any army or air force base anywhere in the United States. The Stars and Stripes stood furled in one holder behind the man at the desk, the unit standard in the other. Only the view out the window of the calm, turquoise, palm-fringed lagoon was unique.

"Where the hell have you two been?"

He was a thin, dapper little man with a fierce gray mustache, narrow blue eyes, and a full uniform with tie and confetti. The booming voice sounded as if it came from a chest three times the size of his.

"We told you that we were checking the reef up off Ebaye, General Scott," Carter said.

"You told me that you were checking the reef yesterday morning, not for twenty-four hours! I don't care who you report to when you're not on Kwajalein, but when you *are* on Kwajalein, you will report to me at least three times a day! I don't like DOD Intelligence or CIA clowns snooping around my command, not to mention foreign agents, unless I know every goddamned thing they're doing every goddamned minute of every goddamned day! Is that clear to you, Commander Carter?" He glared at Carter, then turned his cold eyes to Siobhan. "And to you, Commander O'Neill?"

"If you would let us report, General, maybe you would find out why we didn't report earlier."

The irate general jumped to his feet. "Don't get wise with me, Carter! I know you Intelligence people! You spend half your time making simple problems complicated so you can justify your jobs, and the other half spying on real soldiers! You may be hotshot snoopers, but here you're under my command, you hear?"

"How could we forget?" Carter said drily.

Siobhan O'Neill said, "Would you care to hear what we've really been doing, General Scott, or would you rather rave and rant a bit longer?"

She smiled pleasantly. The general turned slowly, his eyes wide. He was so astonished he opened his mouth and then closed it again without saying another word. Siobhan nodded to Carter.

"You want to give the report, Nelson?"

General Scott blinked, looked from one of them to the other, then slowly sat down again behind his desk and nodded. In a voice that was almost soft he said, "Report, Commander Carter."

Carter sat in a chair facing the general. "We decided to check out the reports of the native divers on Ebaye: the moving 'things' down deep that looked like black cigars. You know that some divers who went down didn't come up. So we dove all along the reef on the ocean side. Most of the day nothing happened. We saw nothing and spotted no danger of any kind."

Siobhan said, "We were just about to give it up, surface, and get back to our boat, when we saw it. Not something small, and not cigar-shaped. Big and more like a whale. A submarine."

"Submarine?" The general sat bolt upright, mustache bristling. "Russian? A Russian sub off Kwaj? I knew it! I've told the Pentagon over and over—"

"More like a submersible," Carter interjected. "For deep-diving research."

"And not Soviet," Siobhán added. "Not from any country I could place."

"It has to be Russian! I've suspected it all along. That surveillance ship out there is only a decoy. The Russians've got subs out there ready to attack at any time."

"I know every sub in the world, General," Siobhán said, "and this one wasn't any Russian type I know."

"Then what type was it, Commander O'Neill?" General Scott snapped.

"No type I'd ever seen before."

"So it could be Russian as well as any country's!"

"Yes," Siobhán admitted. "I can't say for sure it wasn't a new Soviet type."

"The important thing, General," Carter said, "isn't who it belongs to, but what it is. It's smaller and fatter than any attack sub, longer and faster and much larger than any research sub Siobhán or I had ever heard of. It has rows of windows, outside access ports, and divers that don't use air tanks."

The general stared. "That's impossible! All divers use air tanks. I mean, all free divers *have* to use air tanks. They. . . . Divers? What divers?"

Carter went on to tell the general everything about their adventure under the Pacific, including the night stranded on the tiny islet on Bigej Channel—with certain details left out that the general would have considered a gross dereliction of military ethics and duty.

"They tried to kill you?"

"They weren't playing water polo," Carter said.

"And they didn't have air tanks," Siobhán said.

"Impossible," General Scott repeated. "No air tanks and some kind of magnetic force beam? You expect anyone to believe that *Star Wars* claptrap?"

"*Star Trek*," Carter said. "They use tractor and

force beams on *Star Trek*, not in *Star Wars*."

"Whatever," the general snapped.

"*Star Wars* or *Star Trek*, it grabbed us and held us," Siobhan O'Neill said, "and it came from that submersible."

"A magnetic force beam that held our tanks. When we slipped out of the tanks we got away."

"About ten miles out to sea," Siobhan said, "and that's why we didn't report yesterday or last night."

The general ignored her, scowled, and pondered behind his mammoth desk with the turquoise lagoon outside the window behind him. He was the kind of man who never turned to look out at the beauty of the lagoon.

"Those divers," he said suddenly. "The ones you killed. Any chance of getting their bodies? Their equipment? To prove they were Russians?"

"I doubt it," Carter said. "By this time they've floated out to sea if the sharks haven't gotten them."

"Or if that sub hasn't retrieved them," Siobhan said. "I have a suspicion that whoever is running that sub wouldn't want to be identified."

"Russians," the general said. "There's no other possible explanation. And that means they've developed a bunch of new weapons and are waiting right offshore to take over Kwaj any time they want to just as I've been telling Washington for ten years. We must report it at once. Washington can lodge a protest with the U.N. and Moscow within a day. We can show the whole world what sneaky bastards those Russians are." He swiveled in his chair to face his telephone. "I'll expect your full reports in writing on my desk within an hour."

Carter and Siobhan O'Neill did not get up.

"We're not going to report that that sub was Russian, General," Carter said.

"Or that it was or is any threat to this installation," Siobhan added. "That would be unsubstantiated speculation, and we deal in facts, sir."

The general's face turned beet red and then purple.

"You'll report this discussion! That's a fact."

Carter stood up. "You'll have the reports of our investigation in one hour. If that isn't satisfactory, take it up with the Pentagon and Canberra."

The general was still glaring at them in fury as they walked out.

FOUR

Outside in the peaceful Pacific sunlight, Carter and Siobhan O'Neill stood under palm trees and looked out over the glistening lagoon.

"Do you think it's a Soviet action, Nelson?"

"It could be. They've never liked us tracking their satellites from here, and they'd sure want to get their hands on the SDI research data."

"But they've got that surveillance ship right offshore for that."

"We wouldn't send the SDI data out of here. No, they'd have to come in and get that by covert action."

Siobhan watched a small outrigger canoe sailing across the mirrorlike surface of the lagoon. "Then it could be the Soviets."

"I don't know," Carter mused. "It would have to be tended from that surveillance ship—there's no other tender out there. But as far as I can tell, that ship is exactly what it seems to be, not a sub tender."

"It could have a base somewhere on one of the islands."

"Possible, but I'm not sure what a sub could do to get data from onshore. Seems to me a collapsible rubber boat would be a lot better for that. Someone has to

31

come ashore to swipe hard data."

"Then who? What? And how do those divers breathe without air tanks?"

"And who developed that magnetic force beam?"

"Could the Soviets just be testing new weapons?"

"Why pick Kwaj? There's sure to be hell to pay internationally if they're spotted."

"Maybe just because of that. Stir up the waters. American arrogance taking over the whole Pacific."

"Show what they can do?"

"It's possible," Siobhan said.

Carter nodded. "I think we'd better make out our own reports directly, before General Scott files his and doctors ours."

"Agreed. I'll go and code mine now. It should take me about an hour."

"Right," Carter said.

He watched her go along the shaded street that looked more like Kalamazoo than Kwajalein, still wearing only her bikini and carrying her fins, mask, and spear gun. When she was out of sight, Carter slipped back into the headquarters building and found an empty office. He picked up the local intraisland phone and dialed a series of numbers. Beeps and clicks and pings crackled through the instrument, and then a sultry voice came on.

"Hello there, N3, where *are* you calling from? The signal is bouncing off some Soviet satellite. My, my."

It was the secret computer network of AXE that could pick up any telephone signal anywhere, and the sexy electronic voice was David Hawk's little joke.

"Top secret for the director himself. Code One. Killmaster clearance."

Carter was in no mood for making jokes with a computer this morning. After more clicks and pings, the gruff voice of David Hawk came on the line.

"It's two in the morning, N3. It had better be important."

"It's nine in the morning tomorrow here, sir, and it could be."

"I hope it is. That general out there's been burning ears at DOD Intelligence for two weeks. What the hell are you doing to him?"

"Being here," Carter said.

"One of those generals?"

"In spades."

"I'll talk to someone."

"You'd better, or he'll start World War Three."

"Tell me about it. What's happening out there under the ocean?"

Carter told Hawk about the events of the day before, including the divers without air tanks, the strange submersible, and the magnetic force beam. He could hear his Chief's butane lighter snap, the furious puffing to light the omnipresent cheap cigar.

"That's science fiction, N3."

"Not now it isn't," Carter said.

"You sound like you've said that before."

"I have."

"And you probably will again," Hawk growled in far-off Washington. "You think this submersible and those divers are connected to the disappearing Marshall Islanders and the shapes some divers saw down deep outside the reef out there?"

"No proof or even evidence, but it stands to reason there could be some connection."

"Russians?"

"General Scott thinks so," Carter admitted, "but General Scott thinks the Russians are responsible for the common cold and sunspots."

"If not the Soviet Union, then who?"

"Haven't a clue yet. Maybe peace activists or environmental zealots. Greenpeace or some other group. They've been threatening to sail out here and picket the place for years."

"Where would they get a submarine?"

"Where did the Weathermen get guns? There's always someone interested in causing Uncle Sam trouble."

"Killers?" Hawk's voice said after a moment. "Those divers attacked you. Greenpeace has never committed any violence."

"Then it's another group. Nice, normal, peaceful people are bombing abortion clinics."

The distant cigar was puffed furiously. "All right, it's possible, and it would be a lot worse than the Kremlin boys as far as our world image is concerned, not to mention the danger to the secret work out there."

"What danger could a submarine be?" Carter asked. "You can't torpedo an island. They could land and take this island, but they couldn't hold it a week, and what the hell for? What excuse would anyone use?"

"The army's having trouble with the Kwajaleinis. They want a better financial deal from Washington, and they'd just as soon stop the operation and get us off their island. Maybe someone wants to pull a Grenada on us, liberate the Kwajaleinis from our capitalist exploitation."

"Then why kill Kwajaleini divers? *If* the missing ones have been killed."

"Maybe they were people who wouldn't go along with the radicals who want us out. Maybe to scare the hell out of the Kwajaleinis to keep them in line."

Carter thought it over in the silence of the empty office on the peaceful little island lost in the vast Pacific. "They'd have to have a base somewhere. The only possibilities are that Soviet surveillance ship offshore, one of the other islands of the atoll, or one of the other atolls in the Marshall group."

"The ship's too obvious, even if it is a Kremlin operation," Hawk decided. "We can check out the other Marshalls later. Concentrate on the other islands in the Kwajalein atoll."

"You know how many pieces of sand and coral there are in this atoll?"

"Ninety-three," Hawk answered cheerfully. "That's your assignment. You and the Aussie commander. I'll get Canberra to tell her. And try to keep your mind on the submarine base, Killmaster."

Hawk's chuckle was still echoing in Carter's ear as he slowly hung up the receiver and sat staring into space. He had no answers for what the submersible was doing around Kwajalein, or why the divers had tried to kill him and Siobhan, but Hawk was right to be concerned: it had to be there for some reason. And whatever the reason, there had to be a base for service, supply, and repairs. What better place to hide a secret submarine base than among ninety-three sandy islets around the world's largest lagoon?

AXE's premier Killmaster left the empty office and went back out into the bright sunlight baking the tiny island five thousand miles from the homeland it served, a service that did not exactly please its five-thousand-plus rightful owners now crowded into a seventy-eight-acre slum of cement block and plywood shanties on salt-spray-coated Ebaye Island just to the north of the middle-American paradise of Kwajalein itself. Was it possible that someone was working with the disgruntled Kwajaleinis to get their island back? Maybe to use them to create an international incident against the United States?

Still thinking about this, Carter returned to his quarters in the military personnel area and sat down to prepare his official written report as Commander Nelson Carter, Department of Defense Intelligence. It did not take long. He simply reported the facts in detail leaving out the night on the island and any speculations at all. Then he showered and dressed in his navy uniform, and went out again. He walked toward Siobhan O'Neill's quarters. The Australian intelligence officer came out before he got there. She had changed into her tropical uniform and carried her official report.

"What did Canberra say?" Carter asked.

"File the facts, don't speculate, keep my mouth shut,

and let General Scott make a horse's arse of himself.
Not quite in those words, but that was the gist. How
about Washington?''

He had forgotten to contact DOD, but Hawk would
cover that base for him.

"Same," he said. "Had any more thoughts on who's
behind our sub?"

"Greenpeace or the local disgruntleds," she said.
"We have to find where its base of operations is."

She was a very intelligent intelligence officer.

"First we report back to our little Napoleon."

They walked back up the quiet street under the palms,
and the master sergeant outside General Scott's office
grinned at them again.

"Better than bikinis and spear guns. The general will
be pleased."

"Wait until he reads our reports, Sergeant," Carter
said.

The sergeant shrugged. "I don't think he's waiting
for your reports, sir. We got his communiqué off to the
Pentagon half an hour ago."

"Lovely," Siobhan said.

The sergeant announced them again, and they went
in. General Scott was standing at his window this time,
actually looking out at the turquoise lagoon. But he
wasn't seeing it. He was seeing Washington and Moscow and confrontation and maybe another star or two
for him. Seeing such an exciting international confrontation, and such dazzling stars, he didn't even turn as
Carter and Siobhan came in.

"Just leave the reports on my desk. There's no hurry
now."

"What does that mean, General?" Siobhan said.
"I've made my report to Canberra, and we have orders
to give you our full cooperation."

The general turned. "It means, Commander O'Neill,
that I have made *my* report to Washington and the matter is being taken care of at this moment. Your reports
are no longer of any importance."

"What the hell could you tell Washington without our reports, General Scott?" Carter demanded.

"As your commanding officer, I summarized your verbal reports and presented my conclusions from the data. So Washington already has everything important in your reports. I suggest you relax until I receive further instructions from the Pentagon."

Siobhan stared at the arrogant little general. "You *summarized* our reports? You mean you—"

"Lied," Carter snapped. "You reported your own conclusions and not ours."

"You told Washington the sub and divers were Soviet?" Siobhan cried.

"Without saying that we don't think they are a Soviet operation?" Carter added.

The general bristled. "They *are* Soviet! They can't be anything else. That is my analysis, and that was my report." He looked at his watch and smiled grimly. "At this moment Washington is filing an official protest with the Soviet government and the United Nations Security Council. We'll see how those damned Russians try to lie their way out of this."

Carter and Siobhan O'Neill looked at each other, then at the belligerent little general.

"And if they aren't Soviet?" Carter said.

"What do you think the Kremlin will do, General?" Siobhan said.

"If they aren't, we'll apologize," General Scott said.

"I hope we have time," Carter said.

Siobhan turned. "Maybe there's still time for my people to contact Washington and Moscow and give our reports, Nelson."

"There isn't," the general said, "and all outgoing communications have now been shut down. Kwajalein is under a state of emergency."

"On whose authority?" Carter demanded.

"The commanding general's!"

He grinned at them, enjoying his triumph and his power.

"I hope you've got plenty put away for your retirement to the farm, General," Carter said. "When it turns out not to be the Soviets, you'll be on half pay for a long time."

"When it *is* the Russians, and we catch them red-handed, there'll be a star for me, Carter, not retirement. Maybe two more stars."

"Is that what really matters, General?" Siobhan said quietly.

The general flushed angrily. "No! My duty is what is important, and I know my duty if you two don't! Now, I want you—"

"*You can't go in there, Sam!* The general's busy!"

"Must talk! Big trouble."

The voices came from outside, in front of the general's office. The voices of the master sergeant and someone else were loud enough to come right through the closed door.

"You'll just have to. . . . Sam! Goddamnit, don't you try to—Sam!"

The outer door burst open, and a short, dark, white-haired Kwajaleini wearing nothing more than a wraparound, skirtlike cloth and a mother-of-pearl and coral necklace came into the office with the master sergeant behind him trying to grab his arm and pull him back out.

"General, boss! Must talk. Very bad trouble!"

General Scott scowled at the distraught Kwajaleini. "Dammit, Sam, I've told you before! All your problems and complaints must be submitted to my office in writing. I have more important matters than your complaining on my mind."

"No complaining. My people dying. On beach. Six die this morning! Go into lagoon—"

The general blinked. "Dying?"

"On beach. They dive. They come out of lagoon. They die. You come, bring help, tell Washington. Something you do in water! Your bombs. Your big rockets. One hit in lagoon this morning. Now my people die! What you do to lagoon?"

"Ridiculous!" General Scott snapped. "Nothing we've done could kill anyone. Your divers must be . . . the Russians!" The general whirled on Carter and Siobhan O'Neill. "They're putting something in the lagoon! That's what they're up to! Poisoning the lagoon so they can take over the base! I knew it!"

Carter headed for the door. "Maybe we should go and see what *is* happening before we decide who's doing it."

The Kwajaleini, Sam, nodded eagerly. "You come. Bring medicine. Doctors. Hurry!"

General Scott glared at Carter, but he finally nodded. "Very well. Sergeant, alert the medical office and prepare a launch to go up to Ebaye."

FIVE

Led by General Scott's second in command, a Major Hammond, the launch carrying a squad of six soldiers, with Carter and Siobhan aboard, plowed through the calm, crystal-clear, green-blue waters of the great lagoon toward the island of Ebaye to the north where all five thousand Kwajaleinis had been moved by army orders.

"The general thinks there's a Soviet operation going on," Major Hammond said. "Would you know about that, Commander Carter?"

"We know about it," Carter said.

Major Hammond frowned. "You think it could mean real trouble?"

"If your general has his way, it could," Siobhan O'Neill said.

"Yeah." Major Hammond nodded. "The general does worry me sometimes, the way he hates the Russians."

"You don't want trouble, Major?" Siobhan said.

"No, ma'am. I don't think anyone in his right mind does."

Carter watched the tall, slender major. An unusual professional soldier. Maybe there was some hope.

The launch plowed on through the bright, turquoise water of the vast lagoon, past deserted islets, until the larger island of Ebaye came into sight with its crowded shantytowns where the Kwajaleinis lived. Carter thought about the possibility of them being connected to the submersible and the attacking divers. He was aware that there were many among them not at all sure, considering the way things had turned out for them, that they were glad the Americans and not the Japanese had won World War II.

"Major!"

"Commander?"

The helmsman was staring down into the water behind the launch, and the bowman was doing the same. It was the bowman who spoke.

"There's a ton of seaweed down under here, sir. I never saw any seaweed in this part of the lagoon."

"It could foul the propellor even with the guard we've got," the helmsman said, staring down into the water that was suddenly no longer crystal clear. No longer turquoise. It was dull blue with great dark shadows underneath, dark, twisting shadows under the surface of the lagoon that seemed to move.

Shadows that *did* move!

"There must be a strong current through here," Siobhan said as she stared down, the launch moving more slowly now as it had to cut through the thick vegetation under the surface.

"There's no current," Carter said. "That weed is growing so fast we can see it grow! It's not being moved. It's moving on its own. Growing!"

Everyone stared down at the water as the launch slowly moved next to the rickety pier on Ebaye Island where a large delegation of the Kwajaleinis were waiting for them. It looked as if most of the population of the island was ranged behind along the lagoon beach. The Kwajaleini leader, Sam, was the first to jump ashore.

"You come," he said back over his shoulder to

Carter and Siobhan and Major Hammond as he strode along the pier to the beach and turned toward a small shanty close to the beach. They followed, the squad of soldiers close behind them.

Sam opened the shanty door and they all had to duck to go in. The piercing sound of female voices weeping and wailing greeted them as they entered.

"Stay around the building," Major Hammond instructed his soldiers.

Inside the shanty the light was dim; the sunlight struggled through two small dirty windows. But Carter, Siobhan, and the major didn't need a lot of light to see what was in the hut.

The bodies of six young Kwajaleini men were laid out on makeshift biers of boards and palm fronds. Their faces were contorted like the faces of poison victims. Around them some ten or twelve women, young and old, cried and shrieked, tearing at their hair and touching the dead men.

"We find all on beach today. All on lagoon. Two maybe mile from other three. All okay yesterday. No sick. Young and strong. All divers, very good swimmer. Two more very sick, not die. Ask what happen. Nothing, they say. Nothing happen. Only dive, swim, come up, nothing happen until come to shore and get sick."

"Where are the two sick ones?" Major Hammond asked.

"In hospital down Kwajalein. Doctors say not know what sickness is."

Carter, Siobhan, and Major Hammond examined the six dead youths.

"Not a mark on these two," Carter said.

"Nor these," Siobhan said.

"No marks on any of them," Major Hammond realized. "Not even a bruise."

"Then how did they die?" Siobhan wondered.

"Drowned?" Major Hammond suggested.

Chief Sam said, "No drown. Swim too good. Drowned man not look like that."

"More like poison," Carter said. "We'll have to have autopsies, Major."

The major nodded. "I'll have the bodies transported down to Kwaj, and we'll get a navy pathologist to fly in from Pearl."

"Meanwhile," Siobhan said, "what about that stuff growing out there in the lagoon?"

Carter turned to Sam. "When did you first notice that weed out in the lagoon?"

"No see. Not there yesterday."

"You mean you didn't notice it until today?"

"See today. Not see yesterday. Not there yesterday."

Major Hammond tried to explain things to the Kwajaleini leader. "No, it had to be there yesterday, probably for a few weeks at least, but you simply didn't notice it, Chief. It was probably down deep and grew up toward the surface where you spotted it today. Seaweed that thick must have taken years to grow."

Sam shook his head emphatically. "Dive two days before. No weed. No weed ever. Now weed all over."

"Impossible!" the major said.

Carter said, "Maybe we'd better take another look at that weed, Major. Something killed these six divers, and the seaweed seems to be a mystery. When you've got two mysteries, there's a hell of a good chance there's some kind of connection."

"Commander Carter's right," Siobhan said. "We'd better get some samples of that weed and have it analyzed along with the autopsy on these poor men."

The major nodded, and they all filed silently out of the makeshift morgue leaving the weeping and wailing women with their dead men. Outside, the Kwajaleinis were still all standing on the lagoon beach, staring at the water, watching the shanty apprehensively.

Leaving the squad of soldiers onshore to guard against any sudden attack from lagoon or ocean, Major Hammond, Carter, and Siobhan O'Neill reboarded the launch, and the navy men turned it back out into the lagoon.

"Let's see the extent of the seaweed first," Carter suggested.

Major Hammond nodded, and gave the orders to the helmsman. In the bow, the crewman used a long pole to push aside the thick weed breaking the surface now and threatening to foul the propellor and climb up the sides of the launch itself. To Carter, it seemed like hundreds of snakes slithering out of the now dark water of the lagoon.

"Good thing we've got a weed-protection cage around the prop, Major," the helmsman said. "I just hope it's good enough to keep out this much junk."

"My God," the major whispered. "You really can see it grow. Where the hell could it have come from?"

"Yeah," Carter said. "Where and how?"

Siobhan looked at him. "Are you thinking what I think you're thinking?"

Carter nodded. "Two mysteries could be a coincidence, but when you have *three* mysteries, something begins to smell very peculiar, wouldn't you say, Commander?"

"But what could that submersible have to do with a lagoon full of seaweed and some dead divers? Coincidence or connection?" Siobhan wondered aloud.

"Here's the edge, sir!" the bowman called out.

The launch seemed to surge ahead as it broke clear of the darker water where the plants were growing. Out in the open lagoon, the turquoise water was crystal clear again. They were almost a mile from shore, and as Carter looked down into the depths with the sand sparking below, he could see the water darken far down even as he watched.

"You can see it growing out," he said, his voice shaking a little in disbelief.

They all peered down into the crystalline depths in silence as the strange weed seemed to flow out from its own dark shadow into the clear water and then upward toward the surface. The helmsman turned to move with it, and slowed the launch until it was moving at the same pace as the growing weed.

"It's growing at almost five knots an hour, Major," he said, his voice awed.

"All right," Major Hammond said. "Turn her around, and let's head back to shore and pick up those bodies to take down to Kwaj. I've already radioed the general to have the navy fly in a pathology team."

The launch turned smartly in the clear water, then plunged back into the dark morass where the weed had grown so thick it was like entering a swamp, the helmsman weaving slowly to keep the propellor cage clear, the crewman at the bow pushing aside the thicker stems with a long pole.

"Whatever it is, it doesn't seem to grow up onto the shore," Siobhan O'Neill pointed out. "Just in the lagoon, heading out toward the center."

"Maybe—" Carter began.

The horrible cry of agony and terror came from the bow of the slowly moving launch.

The bow crewman had leaned too far over to clear his pole of weeds, had fallen overboard, and had climbed back in laughing. He was wet all over with lagoon water, and long strands of the thick weed hung from him.

Now he stood with screams coming from his gaping mouth, his whole body rigid and trembling in one great spasm like a man bitten by the deadliest of snakes.

"What is it?" Siobhan O'Neill cried.

The third crewman ran to his comrade and reached to take the seaweed off the screaming, shivering man.

"No!" Carter shouted. "Don't touch him! Don't touch that weed!" He turned to Siobhan and Major Hammond. "It's the water. The weed. That's what killed those divers. The weed contains a nerve poison, and it makes the whole lagoon poisonous."

The third crewman jumped back away from the violently trembling man. And even as they watched, the screaming sailor fell to the bottom of the launch, his mouth still open but emitting no sound now, his eyes staring emptily into the bright sky above the sparkling lagoon. He was dead.

"My God . . ." Major Hammond breathed.

"I . . . I saw a guy die like . . . like that on New Guinea once," the helmsman said from behind them all, his voice shaking in the silent sunlight of the beautiful Pacific day. "He got a snake bite, and he died just like that. Shaking and screaming. It took just seconds. All shaking and screaming and then nothing. In seconds—I mean, maybe a couple of seconds and it's all over, you know?"

"All right, sailor," Carter said. "Don't anyone touch him, and get us back to shore fast."

The helmsman nodded, and the launch plowed through the weed as fast as it could with the once clear water of the lagoon as thick as a swamp now. No one spoke. They kept staring at the dead man lying in the sun with his empty eyes and gaping mouth. On shore the Kwajaleinis were still lined up along the dazzling white beach with the green palms behind them and their shacks scattered around the salt-drenched little slum of an island. Only their chief, Sam, stood on the pier.

As the launch approached the pier, some of the younger men started to trot toward the water as if to come out and help pull it into shore.

"No!" Carter shouted. "Everyone stay away from the lagoon! Don't touch the water!"

"Stay back!" Major Hammond yelled. "Sam! Keep your people far back from the lagoon! Don't touch the water yourself!"

On the pier, Sam turned to order his young men back away from the lagoon, repeating the warning from the launch. As the launch touched the pier, Carter was the first ashore, with Siobhan behind him. Sam waited on the pier for them, his face expressionless.

"We believe you now, Sam," Carter said grimly. "That weed wasn't there yesterday. I think it just killed one of our navy men, and I think it's what killed your divers. It's growing fast enough to see. At this rate it'll choke the whole lagoon in days, eventually the whole ocean. Maybe that'll take years, even centuries, but if it isn't stopped, it'll fill all the oceans of the world."

Sam remained impassive. "You find way to stop?"

"First we've got to find out what it is, how it got in the lagoon, and where it came from," Carter said. "Meanwhile, you have to stay out of the lagoon, and I wouldn't go into the ocean until we can check it. Keep your people away even from the shoreline. Do you understand? No one should get near that weed at all. Don't touch it, and don't even breathe near the shore."

Sam nodded. "No go near water or shore. How long?"

"I don't know yet."

"Not long. Must dive, fish. Need to eat."

"We'll have a team up here to check the ocean in an hour. They'll check the whole shoreline. I want you and your people to watch the lagoon shore. Make sure none of that seaweed comes ashore. It doesn't look like it grows on land, but we have to be certain. Check the ocean side too. If you see any sign of weed in the ocean, report to me or Commander O'Neill or Major Hammond."

Sam nodded. "What you do now?"

"Report to General Scott," Carter said grimly. "Then we'll start to work to find out what this weed is, how to stop it, and what, or who, is behind it."

SIX

The slow-moving launch and its grisly cargo broke out of the weed to the south less than a mile north of Kwajalein Island, the dark green shoots of the weed seeming to follow it south like the heads of a million snakes emerging from the water behind.

"It'll be around Kwaj itself in less than a day," Major Hammond said. "What if it comes ashore?"

"I don't think it will," Carter said. "Strange and impossible as it is, it seems to be just a water plant that can't live out of water."

"Strange and impossible," Siobhan O'Neill said. "Like science fiction."

"Yeah," Carter said. "The third time in two days. There has to be a connection, Siobahn."

"I'd say ninety-ten for," she said.

"Which leaves us to figure out who, how, what, and why."

"After we try to explain it to General Scott."

"That," Major Hammond said, "isn't going to be easy."

They landed at the main dock of the tree-shaded island where a team of corpsmen from the hospital met them to take the seven bodies to the morgue. The pathologists were still on their way from Pearl Harbor and wouldn't arrive for some hours, if not as late as the next morning.

Carter and Siobhan O'Neill went with the bodies to the hospital. There they met with the technicians in its small but well-equipped and advanced laboratory. News of the disaster on Ebaye had preceded the launch party back to Kwajalein, and the technicians and doctor in charge were ready to help.

"We'll need samples of the lagoon water in the weed and out in the clear," Carter explained. "And samples of the weed itself: leaves, shoots, stalks. Wear full protective clothing as if you were dealing with radioactive material. Do you have it?"

"We have it," the chief pharmacist said. "Every navy installation has. Nuclear ships could have trouble anywhere."

"Use long poles to gather the seaweed, and use scoops on the ends of poles to get the water. Don't touch *anything*—even with protective gloves. Not until we know a lot more."

"Roger," the officer agreed.

"What do we do when we get the stuff back here?" the doctor asked.

"Any test you can think of, especially for poisons, probably nerve poisons, plus every botanical detail to try to identify the plants. But do it all in a glove box, and don't touch the stuff even with the rubber gloves. Forceps, sticks, but not hands."

"I hope it's not really that serious," the doctor said.

"I hope so too, but we'd better get the pathology report and some idea of what we're dealing with before we take any chances at all."

Carter and Siobhan left the lab team preparing to go to the launch and make the trip to Ebaye to collect their samples. Then they went to report to General Scott. Major Hammond had already given his report. The red color of the general's face and his ramrod stance in front of his desk, hands clasped behind him, didn't bode well for a reasonable analysis of the situation facing them.

"Seven casualties! Seven! And one is even an American! You still think the Russians aren't behind it? And what can you tell me about how it happened? Nothing, I'll bet. Intelligence! I tell you, it was intelligence that cost us our win in Vietnam. Well?"

Carter explained about the thick, growing weed, and the unmarked deaths, and his suspicions.

"Poisonous seaweed that grows at more than five knots an hour?" The general stared at all three of them, then turned to Siobhan O'Neill. "You agree with these two, Commander O'Neill? That's what you saw?"

"I saw the weed, but I can't prove yet that it caused the deaths. But I watched the crewman die, General, and it certainly looked like it was the weed or the water or both, and it acted like a poison."

The general began to pace his silent office as the other three watched him. "Biological warfare, that's what it is! I've always known they were working on it, but I never suspected they would use it." He turned to face them all. "It's a sneak attack, just like Pearl Harbor! We have to move fast. I'll contact Washington immediately. You three—"

"A sneak attack on six native divers and ninety-three piles of sand, General?" Siobhan cut in. "Wouldn't you say that was exposing their hand for very little gain?"

Carter was thoughtful. "This is the main tracking station for keeping an eye on Soviet satellites. Possibly they want to knock out our tracking eyes because they have something going on up in space they don't want spotted too soon."

The general grunted. "I see one of you is doing a little clear thinking at least. This is precisely the first installation they would knock out if they were launching a satellite attack, and I'll bet my britches that's just what they're doing!"

"Sir," Major Hammond said nervously, "the, er,

seaweed and all isn't going to knock out our radar tracking very fast. I mean, if they wanted to mount a surprise attack to cover satellite operations, wouldn't they have hit the radomes and installations first? Hard and fast . . . sir?"

"The weed is just preparation, you idiot! Softening us up. Fooling us. We think there's some natural disaster going on, and we get all involved in it, see? Then, while we're running around looking at stupid plants, that submarine sneaks in, lands divers, and knocks out the whole installation! Only they're not fooling me, and we'll be ready for them!"

The stubborn general continued pacing around his office. The brilliant Pacific sun was bright outside, and the clear water of the lagoon sparkled through the palm trees. But the dazzling turquoise color was already darkening to the north where the weed advanced southward. "Washington will get paratroopers here in a matter of hours. We'll have all the carriers in the Pacific diverted, every missile cruiser. Hunter subs should reach us from Guam inside half a day. If they just give us a little time! Just half a day, that's all I need." He turned on Siobhan O'Neill. "What about your forces, Commander? How soon can you get paratroopers up here? Maybe some cruisers?"

Siobhan just stared at the general. "I made my report, sir. In my opinion the submersible and divers were not Soviet, therefore the weed and deaths are not caused by the Soviet Union. My government isn't going to move a Boy Scout on your call without word from me or definite proof that the Soviet Union, or any other enemy power, is behind the events here."

The general turned beet red. "Major Hammond, place Commander O'Neill under immediate arrest! I'm beginning to think she may be an enemy agent. New Zealand is in Moscow's pocket, why not Australia?"

"You'd better arrest me, too, General," Carter said. "The report I filed said the same thing. I don't think

Washington's going to move the Pacific fleet on just your word.''

"You think the report of a two-bit DOD Intelligence agent is going to be taken over *my* report?" The feisty little martinet laughed. "They'll have a division of jumpers down here before we finish talking! Now—"

The outer door of the office was flung open, and General Scott's master sergeant burst in, pale and excited. "General—!"

"What the hell do you think you're doing, Sergeant? You don't just—"

"Sir! It's the Russians! That ship they've got out there? They're broadcasting. Calling to us. I mean, they're on open band, sir! They're talking right out on open band, calling for help!"

General Scott stood rigid. "Help? Calling *us*? They've never. . . . They're not even supposed to be . . ."

"Maybe we'd better hear what they're saying, General," Major Hammond suggested nervously.

Carter and Siobhan were already on their way to the door. The general blinked, stared at Carter and Siobhan, then at the sergeant and Major Hammond. Then he nodded.

"Yes. The radio room. Of course. Follow me," he said as he walked out of the office behind Carter and Siobhan, the major and the sergeant following him.

They hurried along the corridor of the headquarters building to the large communications room where the base kept in touch with the entire world and the satellites in space. Three radiomen were all grouped around the main speaker console listening to a scared, angry, baffled, terrified voice speaking in excellent English.

"Mayday! Mayday! Come in, Kwajalein. Soviet electronic surveillance ship fifteen miles offshore due northeast. Come in, Kwajalein! What are you doing to us? We lodge official, formal protest. You are using biological warfare that is specifically forbidden by all international agreements and common humanity! Whatever you are doing, you must stop! We surrender! Send help at once! Stop your attack! We capitulate! Urgent medical aid needed and evacuation of ship. Coordinates—''

Carter pushed the radioman aside and took up the microphone. ''Kwajalein responding to mayday of Soviet surveillance ship. Nelson Carter, Department of Defense Intelligence. If you have KGB aboard, put him on. Inform him code DD-three.''

The general was pale as he stared at the speaker as if he could see the face of the Russian. ''It's a trick! To gain time, divert us. Carter, how dare—''

A new voice, in much more Russian-accented English, came over the speaker. ''What do you want, Carter? Is not your inhuman attack enough—?''

''Identify!'' Carter snapped.

There was a silence. Then, ''Major Mishkin, four-four-four-three.''

Carter had no time to check the AXE computer now. He just hoped his challenge had been enough to make the Russian give his true identity. ''What's going on out there, Mishkin?''

''You know what is going on here, Commander. Your biological attack has already killed four of our crew. The ship is immobilized. In the name of humanity we request helicopters to remove us before the ship is dragged under.''

''Seaweed?'' Carter said grimly into the microphone. ''Seaweed growing so thick and fast you can see it? Some of your men attempted to clear it away and died almost at once?''

''You want a testimonial to the efficiency of your inhuman weapon, Carter?'' the KGB voice said bitterly. ''Tell us how long before the weed grows up over the whole ship.''

''It won't. Or we don't think it will. When did you see it first?''

There was another silence. "This morning. We sent divers down to see how deep it went. They did not come back." The voice hesitated. "You are telling us you have not done this, yet you know—"

"It's happening here, Major. The seaweed is filling the whole lagoon. We've lost six native divers and one navy crewman up on Ebaye. We can see the weed advancing on Kwajalein itself right now. Have you made any sighting of unknown divers or an unidentified submersible?"

"It happens there too?"

"Believe me, Major."

The first voice came back on. "This is Commander Karenin. You are telling us that this weed is growing on the atoll too? You are not responsible? Then who is?"

"Our general thinks you are, Commander. What about—"

General Scott raged in the large radio room. "It's all a trick, Carter! I can smell it. They never tell the truth. They're trying to lure our helicopters out there, cripple our defense capability, catch us unawares. You're trafficking with the enemy, playing into their hands, you fool!" He grabbed for the microphone. "Give me that microphone! I'll talk to them the way they have to be talked to!"

Karenin's voice came back on. "Our captain, too, insists it is an American trick, an attack, an attempt to hide from our surveillance a planned surprise attack on our country. What can we do?"

"First, tell me if you've seen any divers or a submersible."

Mishkin answered. "No divers, Carter, but our sonar has picked up a submarine. We consider that it is one of yours."

"Moves too slowly for an attack sub and too fast for a research vessel? Has a shape you don't recognize?"

"*Da*, yes. Both true. It is not yours?"

"No. It isn't yours?"

"*Nyet*." The KGB man's voice sounded even more

scared now. An American danger he could deal with, but some unknown attacker? Suddenly the horror of plants that grew into a mass overnight and killed men who touched the water they grew in hit home. "We have tracked the submarine below us many times. It comes sometimes from the direction of the atoll, sometimes from the north. It passes underneath us and suddenly seems to disappear."

"All right. None of us knows what's going on. I suggest—"

General Scott still raged behind him: "They're lying, Carter, d'you hear? I know they're lying. Don't listen to them! We've got to get our call off to Washington. Every second counts, don't you understand? They're trying to fool us, to prevent us from calling in help!"

Carter shook his head. "No, I don't think so, General Scott. I've never thought those divers or that sub were Soviet, and neither does Commander O'Neill. I think I know fear when I hear it. I think they're as startled and confused as we are. They know all we have to do is send a single chopper out there and disprove their story at once. No, the weed is out there, too, and that means someone is attacking us both, and we'd better find out why pretty damned quick!"

"Nelson's right," Siobhan said.

"I agree with them, sir," Major Hammond said.

The general turned on his heel. "Believe what you like, Hammond. I'm in command here, and I'll give the orders. We don't help Russians, and you're all under arrest. Guards!"

Carter spoke quickly into the microphone. "Mishkin! Get in touch with Moscow, or Vladivostok, or wherever you report, and do it fast. Tell them what is happening. All of it. Tell them General Scott here thinks you people are preparing an attack. Keep your crew away from the water, and see if you can get your ship out of those plants."

"I don't think we can get out, Commander," Commander Karenin's voice said. "We've been trying. The weed's got us locked in so thick the propellers won't turn and it feels like we're in a vise."

"Try. If you can't move, sit tight, contact Moscow, and we'll send help as soon as we can. We may have to clear it with Washington over General Scott's head."

"Hurry, Carter," Major Mishkin said grimly. "The pressure on our hull is building fast. Those plants do not climb from the water, but they grow, and grass has the power to destroy steel in the end."

"As fast as we can," Carter said, and stood up. He and Siobhan and Major Hammond faced the general as armed soldiers came running along the hall toward the radio room.

"I don't want to have to hurt anyone, General," Carter said quietly. He checked where Wilhelmina was hidden under his armpit, Hugo silent up his sleeve, Pierre strapped in its place on his thigh.

"Contact Washington first, General Scott," Siobhan said. "Someone will be hurt here, and we're all on the same side."

"Sir," Major Hammond began, "I think—"

"I don't give a damn in hell what you think, Major!" the general roared. "You'll be a civilian after this—if you're not in prison! You three are mutinying against me, and I'm placing you—"

The sound of the violent explosion filled the room, a deep, rumbling roar that came from two places at once: from the open microphone Carter had not turned off, and from some fifteen miles to the northeast of Kwajalein Island.

Their own battle forgotten, they all rushed out into the bright sunlight and stood staring off across the ocean to the northeast.

A giant piller of smoke climbed into the sky from the blue Pacific. From where there could have been nothing to explode except the Soviet ship.

"My God," General Scott said quietly.

SEVEN

"Maybe," Major Hammond said, "it's not the Soviet ship. Maybe it was something else . . ."

Siobhan stared toward the great pillar of smoke still rising into the cloudless sky. "All of them. No one could survive that. How many?"

"A ship that size," Carter said grimly, "two or three hundred."

General Scott's eyes were dazed, uncomprehending. "But . . . but . . . who? I mean . . . what . . . ? It can't be the . . . the Soviet ship. They're attacking us. They have to be, don't you see? They're behind everything. It has to be them. So . . . so . . . . One of our submarines. A torpedo! No, a missile! One of our missile cruisers must be—"

"General," Major Hammond said, his voice shaking, "we'd know if one of our cruisers was anywhere near Kwaj. Or a submarine. It was an unarmed surveillance ship. We wouldn't sink it without warning. We—"

"But Moscow will think so," Carter said. He turned sharply to the general. "You had Washington file that protest against the submersible and divers yesterday. We accused Moscow of mounting an attack on Kwaj, and that ship reported its danger to Moscow! If they didn't have time to report our communication this

59

morning, Moscow is going to think we sank it on the pretext of them attacking us!''

"Good God," Major Hammond breathed, white-faced. "Carter's right!"

"Moscow could think it's the beginning of a first strike!" Siobhan cried.

General Scott blinked, and his dazed eyes cleared suddenly. "You're right! If they're not behind all this, and with that protest we filed, if I were Moscow, that's just what I'd have to think—I'd order an immediate counterstrike. I must reach Washington at once! The President himself!" He turned to the radioman. "Top-priority emergency channel, coded message. Quick!"

"No," Carter said.

"Dammit, Carter!" General Scott shouted. "I'm admitting I was wrong! We have to contact Washington immediately."

"Sooner than that, General, and I can get to the President a lot faster than you can. Everyone leave—"

"Ridiculous!" General Scott snapped. "I have a top-priority channel to the Pentagon. They'll get to the Secretary of Defense at once and he'll get to the President. What could a DOD Commander—"

"Revelation sixteen, sixteen," Carter said. "Number fifty, row seven."

The little general paled and stared at Carter. "Who the hell *are* you?"

"No time, General. I need the room alone. Now!"

The general stared for another second. Two. Then turned sharply. "Out! Everyone! Leave Carter alone. Guards, cover the outside door. Hurry!"

They quickly filed out, with Siobhan watching Carter quizzically, and the general still staring back at the man who had given him the supersecret code words for immediate, unhesitating assumption of command. The door closed, and Carter turned at once to the powerful intercontinental radio and spoke his code words that connected him to the AXE computer, with the override code for immediate attention of the director.

Hawk's voice was on the speaker before the last word

had time to echo. "Here, N3."

"Soviet surveillance ship offshore Kwajalein blown up. Cause unknown. Not, repeat, *not* U.S. action. Ship was in distress, contacted Kwaj base on open channel. We were in communication, were about to go to assistance when she blew. Protest made yesterday by Washington withdrawn. Soviet in no way connected to occurrences around Kwajalein. We are going to immediate assistance of any survivors. Get the President on the hot line to Gorbachev."

"Christ, N3! With that protest yesterday—"

"Yes, sir."

"I hope there's time."

Hawk was gone. Carter sat back, lit a cigarette, and waited. At the very least an ICBM could be on its way to Kwajalein from somewhere in Siberia, or from a Soviet submarine, at that instant. Seconds from destruction of the atoll and everyone on it. Then again, with that perhaps deadly weed growing so fast you could see it, maybe it would be better for the future of the world if an ICBM was on its way. AXE's premier Killmaster shook his head to clear the thought. They would find what was behind the weed, and how to stop it, without wiping out an atoll or anything else.

Hawk's voice was shaky. "Done, N3. The President is talking to Gorbachev right now."

"I hope they can handle it," Carter said.

"So do I, Nick, so do I." The sound of Hawk's butane lighter came across the eight thousand miles, the slow puffing of the cheap cigar. "All right, the whole story. Why was the Soviet ship in distress? What blew it up?"

"I don't know yet what blew it up," Carter said, "but that submersible, and those divers, are also unexplained."

"You smell a connection?"

"Strongly," Carter said drily into the microphone. "But so far it's only a stink, and there's a beauty of a third mystery, sir."

"Yes?"

Carter told him of the trip to Ebaye, the dead divers, the strange weed that was filling the lagoon, and the death of the navy man who'd fallen among the weeds in the water. "And that was what the Soviet ship broke radio silence about. The same weed had grown up all around the ship, and some of their men were dead from touching it."

"In the ocean?"

"That's what they said."

In far-off Washington, Hawk was silent for a long time. Too long.

"Sir?"

The silence went on. Finally Carter heard a long, slow letting out of breath, and Hawk's voice came again. Low and almost empty.

"Water plants you can actually see grow?"

"I know, it's science fiction again, but it's also true again."

There was a sigh in Washington. "I believe you, Nick. Two days ago we got a crazy message from our people in Australia. They had a report from some retired Australian district commissioner up in some god-forsaken cove in New Guinea. It seems the cove where he lived had been completely choked by sea plants in one night. He reported that they grew so fast you could see them grow. He reported that animals swimming through the seaweed died instantly, and dead fish were all over the cove."

It was Carter's turn to be silent. Hawk's voice went on, almost wearily.

"No one believed it, of course. The Australians thought the old commissioner had gone senile, our people reported, and we thought so too. Now, who knows?"

"New Guinea?"

"Two days ago," Hawk said.

"Someone's experimenting?"

"Sounds like that now, doesn't it."

"Any other reports like that?"

"I'm going to run that question through the computer as soon as we're off. Then I'm going to go back to that New Guinea report and give it the full treatment.''

"I'll see what I can dig up around here," Carter said. "We have a couple of survivors who may be able to tell me something. There may be some evidence out where the Russian ship blew.''

As they talked, both men sensed they were waiting for something, waiting for Kwajalein to disappear in a great blue-white flash and a mushroom cloud. Or maybe Washington. Waiting to see if there was going to be a world to try to save. Waiting. Then Hawk's voice suddenly eased, and grew strong again, vigorous.

"Gorbachev accepts our explanation, Nick, and asks that we do what we can to help. They'll have a ship in the area soon, and they'll send a biological warfare expert to confer with General Scott.''

"Good," Carter said quietly.

"Find out what that weed is and what's behind it, and I'll check out New Guinea. Keep out of all the official stuff, understand?''

"I had to reveal my ultrapriority status to Scott."

"He's a hundred percent by the book. He won't talk about it.''

"Siobhan O'Neill was there too."

"That's your problem. Tell her any lie you want.''

"Thanks.''

"I've told you before to keep your mind on business. Go to work, N3.''

In the silent radio room Carter couldn't help grinning. Nothing ever really fazed the old bulldog. He got up and went out into the corridor. The two guards posted at the radio room door looked at him curiously.

"Where did the others go, soldier?''

"The general's office, I think, sir.''

"Thanks.''

He hurried down the corridors to General Scott's office. In it, the general was alone behind his mammoth desk. He looked at Carter stiffly. He wasn't a man who liked to be upstaged or overruled, but he was also a man who had spent his life obeying orders without question when they were backed by ultimate authority.

"The President got through to Gorbachev, and he understands the situation."

The general nodded.

"Moscow is sending a cruiser and a biological warfare expert to confer with you."

The general wasn't so sure about that. "Very well. How much am I to show them?"

"That's up to you, General."

The general's voice was tight. "I see. And you?"

"I have my own special job. I'll be trying to track down what's behind the weed and the submersible. Just ignore me."

"Of course." The general cheered up. "Any help you need?"

"I'll let you know, sir," Carter said. "What's the situation now?"

General Scott leaned forward, brisk again, back in control at least of his own little empire. "Rescue boats and helicopters have been sent out. Search planes are looking for any evidence of that submarine or anything else unusual out there. I'm waiting for the results of the analysis of the weed and water. The pathology team from Pearl will be here in a few hours. Two missile cruisers and a carrier battle group are on their way."

Carter nodded. "That sounds like all bases are covered."

"I think so. We'll be ready for the Soviet ship and their experts. I'll arrange a meeting aboard their ship, and I'll allow their experts to cooperate fully with our pathology and analysis teams. The rest of the base is off limits."

"That's your decision, sir. I'll be in Commander O'Neill's quarters if you need me."

The general was handling all the routine activities efficiently, which gave Carter a free hand to get on with the important work of tracking down the who and what and why of the deadly weed. He left the general happily arranging and planning, and went to Siobhan's quarters.

He found her packing.

"Going somewhere?"

"Ordered back down under."

"Any reason?"

"Reassignment. Ours is not to reason why, mate."
She looked at him. "Who are you, Nelson? Really?"

"Just a scrambler in the trenches, Siobhan, like
you."

"With a priority code that makes a general jump
through a hoop? That's not my kind of trench."

"Does it matter?"

She watched him. "I'm not sure."

"I hope not."

She zipped up her bag. "Well, off to the kangaroos
and koalas. Perhaps we shall run across each other
again, Nels. If that's your name."

"Make it Nick, and I'll see we do."

She smiled. "Nick, then. *Ciao*, mate."

"I'll drive you to the plane."

She nodded. Carter took her bag and went out to
where a soldier in a Jeep was waiting. They drove to the
airstrip. An Australian Air Force jet was on the runway
ready to leave. She faced him.

"It's been exciting . . . Nick."

"Very."

"Come to Sydney. I'll make it worth your while."

"As soon as I can."

"Right."

She kissed him, then ran for the jet. The door closed
and it taxied away down the runway. Carter stayed there
until it stopped, turned, revved up, and made its run
down and up into the blue Pacific sky. Then he turned
and got back into the Jeep.

"The hospital, soldier."

The Jeep drove off. Carter looked back and up into
the sky. The small jet was already a distant speck
against the vast blue.

EIGHT

At the hospital the lab team had returned from gathering the water and weed samples off Ebaye. They were still peeling off the heavy protective clothing, looking at the samples inside the glove box where they handled all toxic and radioactive materials.

"You can see it still growing even after it's been cut," the chief pharmacist's mate said, staring in at the thick green plant samples that squirmed almost like snakes in their water-filled glass sample bottles. "Up at Ebaye it's a mile out into the lagoon already. It'll be down here at Kwaj in another couple of days."

"Any evidence yet what it is—what kind of poison's involved?" Carter asked.

The laboratory doctor shook his head. "We've run a few preliminary tests on the water, but there's nothing familiar yet."

"The plants look like some edible seaweeds they've been working on up in Japan," one of the technicians said, "but there's some strange differences in the leaf pattern I can't identify. They act like a normal species, only incredibly stronger and faster growing."

"There's a kind of seed pod I've never seen on a plant like these," the second technician said, his voice both worried and excited. The scientist in him was excited by the new, the unexplained, the abnormal—something to be studied and codified.

Carter left them eagerly starting to work on the samples of water and still growing vegetation, handling everything inside the glove box with mechanical instruments and forceps.

He went down to the office of the hospital director. The director was a navy doctor who jumped up as soon as he saw Carter. General Scott had obviously passed the word around that Carter was to get VIP treatment all the way.

"How can I help you, Commander?"

"You've got two Kwajaleini divers in here who came out of the water up on Ebaye sick but alive?"

"We do," the doctor said, shaking his head. "No visible injuries of any kind, no poisons that show up in our tests, but one of them is critical and the other's not far behind."

"Can I see them?"

The doctor hesitated. He had his orders, but he had his ethics, too.

"It could be vital, Doctor," Carter said. He had his job, and there wasn't much room for ethics.

"Very well," the doctor said. General Scott was more important at the moment than Hippocrates.

They went along the clean, silent corridors to a wing where a stern-looking nurse sat at a desk that blocked the corridor. Behind her Carter saw the Kwajaleini leader, Sam, seated outside a room with a closed door.

"Commander Carter will speak with our patients, Mrs. Castro."

The grim nurse looked him up and down. General Scott wouldn't carry a lot of weight with her. But a doctor did. Everything is relative.

"Yes, sir. But there's only one patient. The other died an hour ago."

The doctor shook his head. "Which one?"

"How would I know? It's on the chart."

The old Kwajaleini chief, Sam, stood, then walked to them.

"It was Tevake," Sam said. "The son of my cousin. He has a wife, three children. They will be empty now. We will all be empty now."

"I'm sorry, Sam," the doctor said.

"But you will not leave."

"That's not up to us, Sam."

"Who then is it up to? You are not a free people?"

"We're a big country, Sam. We elect our leaders, and they must do what they think is best for us."

"Who watches them, tells them what is best for you?"

The nurse said, "Sir, we're busy here. We don't have time for people to stand around and talk."

Sam looked at her. "We do not have time *not* to stand and talk."

The Kwajaleini turned away and went back to his seat outside the closed door. The nurse glared after him. The doctor motioned Carter to follow him, and they went to the closed door. Sam stood to go in with them.

"The man is Marave," Sam said. "He was in your navy."

Inside the silent hospital room the slender man lay rigid in the hospital bed, eyes open and staring. Unseeing eyes that stared up at the blank ceiling. Stared but didn't look, the sick man's gaze turned inward.

"Marave?" Sam said gently.

There was no response. The man just lay there, his eyes empty and distant at the same time, not a mark or bruise on him, hands rigid at his sides.

"Can you tell us what happened?" Carter asked.

"In the water," the doctor said. "In the lagoon."

The man's eyes blinked, and his whole body twitched in a sudden spasm. His eyes rolled in his head. His fists clenched. He remained that way, as if frozen in the violent spasm.

"It was the word *water*," the doctor said. "Water, Marave. What happened in the water?"

The man remained rigid. Sam stepped closer to the bed. He said something in Kwajaleini. The man jerked as if stung, cringed, and put his hands up to shield his face. He began to shout in his native language.

"What's he saying?" Carter said quickly.

Sam translated, his face expressionless: "Weed! Weed! Growing! Spit! Spit! Sting. Pots. Spitting pots. Damned pots all over lagoon. Spitting. Growing. Bubbles. Bubbles. Spit. Growing. Growing . . . and he just goes on like that. Talks about pots, spitting, growing, bubbles, weed. He in pain, but not very bad pain. He just talk, talk. Crazy talk."

"Delirious, Carter," the doctor said. "I'm afraid whatever he says isn't reliable."

"That depends. Images can be very reliable if you know how to analyze them. I'll be back later. Sam, can you get me up to Ebaye?"

"You like canoe ride?"

"I like." At the moment it was better than using any official vehicles or aircraft. Slow but alone, and he didn't want any official eyes from any side. You never knew who was behind something as crazy as this.

They left the hospital together, Sam and Carter, and walked along the mid-American street to the docks on the lagoon side where all the electronics whizzes kept their sailboats and powerboats and water skis, the town dock of any affluent East Coast township. Sam's outrigger was tied up at the end of a rickety native pier. The Kwajaleinis had been building canoes the same way when landlocked Europeans were still watching in fear for raiding Viking longships. The outrigger could sail and paddle rings around the European ships that found them, and could still outpaddle and outsail most small boats.

Sam paddled out into the still clear lagoon, then set his sail and the canoe shot forward, skimming the surface of the crystal-clear water. Less than halfway from Kwajalein to Ebaye the water began to darken, and soon the shoots of the thick weed began to break the surface like the heads of snakes swimming inexorably south. The outrigger slowed, but not much, actually sliding ahead on the thick weed itself.

"Lean to right, hold outrigger high," Sam instructed.

Carter leaned. Sam watched the outrigger as loops of the thick weed seemed to grab at it. The canoe itself was too high in the bow for the weed to impede it, but the outrigger could be caught, the boat stopped and turned if not capsized. The two men kept a delicate balance between putting too much weight on the opposite side of the canoe from the outrigger and letting the outrigger fall too deeply into the grasping weed.

Balanced, they seemed to sail even faster over the matted weed so thick Carter felt they could almost walk on it. Eerily deserted, the lagoon stretched empty where normally canoes would be sailing everywhere, the extent of the weed visible in all directions like a dark stain spreading evilly across the turquoise water of the vast lagoon.

When they sailed into the rickety pier on Ebaye, the pier and the beach and even the visible houses were deserted. Sam tied up and they climbed carefully up onto the pier.

"Where does Marave live?" Carter asked Sam.

The Kwajaleini leader led the way up the beach and through the palms to a particularly well-kept cement-block shack with a tin roof. A brisk Caucasian woman in her thirties worked in a thriving vegetable garden behind the shack. She sat back on her heels and wiped her sweating brow as she looked up at Sam. She smiled, but her eyes didn't.

"Any news, Sam?" she asked quietly.

"He same, Lyda," Sam replied. "Commander Carter want talk to you, ask question."

She glanced at Carter. "What questions, Commander?"

"You're not Kwajaleini, Mrs. Marave?"

"Yes, I am," she said. "I married Marave, so I became Kwajaleini. It's quite an education to be on the other side when the Pentagon wants something. It changes one's views after ten years in the navy."

"Did it change your husband's views?"

"Oh, yes. Very much."

"What was he in the navy?"

"What else, Commander? A frogman. Diving is what a Kwajaleini does best."

Frogman? "Did he ever leave the island, Mrs. Marave?"

"Not in years. The navy wanted to set us up on Kwaj because of me, right? But we said no. Not until we can all move back and live on the island that is ours. The only thing Marave kept from the navy is his wet suit. That's almost part of him by now."

"Wet suit?" Carter said. "Your husband wears a wet suit to dive in? Still? I mean, now? The day he got sick?"

"Yes," she said.

A wet suit!

"The other diver," Carter said, turning quickly to Sam. "The other one who was in the hospital. Was he wearing a wet suit?"

"He wear suit."

"Where is Marave's wet suit?" Carter asked.

"In the house," Lyda Marave said.

"Can I see it?"

"It's all in his room," she said, turning back to her garden. "For when he comes home."

Carter went inside. There were only two rooms. The bedroom was neat, almost Spartan. A complete wet suit and diving gear were laid neatly on a long low table near the only window. Carter examined each piece in turn: full two-piece wet suit including feet and head; rubber gloves; fins; watertight join of top and bottom of suit; face mask. The entire outfit was watertight except perhaps for tiny leaks around the mask—and the fact that the mask would have been dipped in the water before being put on.

But no water would have entered beyond the residue of wetting, and some tiny seepage around the mask. The power of the poison in the weed came from contact with the skin, and the wet suit had protected Marave and the second diver who had survived until a few hours earlier. He went back out to where Sam still stood over the working Lyda Marave.

"The other diver, Tevake—is his wet suit on the island?"

Sam nodded, then said something to Lyda Marave in Kwajaleini. She smiled and kept on gardening.

"Thanks, Mrs. Marave," Carter said.

"Will it help Marave?" she said.

"I hope so."

She nodded and went on digging, turning the earth that had to have been brought in from somewhere else.

Sam led Carter to another shack, silent and empty. Tevake's family was gone now. Inside the shack they found the wet suit flung in a heap on the floor, everyone afraid to come near it after the deaths. Carter examined it using the rubber gloves he'd brought with him.

"Where are the gloves?" he asked Sam.

"No gloves. Tevake not like gloves."

Everything else was watertight. But Tevake had not worn gloves. So the potency of the poison in the water was directly proportional to how much skin area it touched. That didn't mean the plants themselves weren't more deadly if touched directly; Carter had no way of knowing if either diver had touched the plants.

"You want to take me back to Kwaj, Sam?" Carter asked.

"No can. Must stay. You take canoe."

Carter nodded, and the two men left the ramshackle home of the dead diver and walked back through the crowded slum of Ebaye to the lagoon and the pier. Sam pointed to a smaller canoe up on land, and the two of them carried it out onto the pier and lowered it carefully into the water, making sure they did not splash themselves or touch the deadly water.

"No take chances," Sam warned. "Not fall into water."

"You can bet on it, Sam," Carter said and grinned.

In the canoe, he paddled out carefully through the thick weed, wearing his rubber gloves, until it was far enough out to set the sail. Balancing far over, coming too close to the lethal water even for him, he sailed south again through the matted weed. To be safe, he sailed far out beyond the weed this time, and circled wide through the clear water toward Kwajalein. He was not the sailor Sam was, and he couldn't afford to make any mistakes.

The long curve to avoid the weed took much more time, and it was evening when Carter finally reached Kwaj through the clear, weed-free water of the lagoon. He went straight to headquarters. General Scott was somewhere at sea meeting with the Soviet experts on their cruiser. Only Major Hammond was in his office, and he told Carter what had happened while he was away.

"We searched the whole area, air and sea, and didn't find any survivors from the Soviet ship. No clues as to what blew her up, either." Hammond shook his head. "The weed is very thick out there. It just seems to be spreading like wildfire. We spotted dead fish, some porpoises, even a whale. If it goes on unchecked . . ." The major only shook his head again.

"What about the pathology team from Pearl?"

"They're working on the bodies. No report yet."

Carter nodded, then went to the laboratory at the hospital. The chief pharmacist's mate shrugged.

"Not a damned thing so far, sir. Whatever the poison is, we can't fit it into anything we know yet. It may not even be a poison, just some reaction of the human body to the seaweed."

"Have you identified the plant?"

"Only that it's some mutant of a common seaplant often used for food in the Far East. We have no clue as to what made it mutate, or how it got into the lagoon or the ocean."

"What about the pathologists? Have they said anything yet about the actual physical cause of death?"

"No, sir. But unofficially they say it looks like a pure case of nerve poisoning, but they have no identification of the type of poison yet. It's like a snake venom, one of them told me, but not from any snake they can classify so far."

Carter left the laboratory and went along toward the

room where the surviving Kwajaleini, Marave, was. If he could get the diver to tell him more about the "spitting pots" and the "bubbles," he might have something to go on. If Marave could talk about exactly what he had done that day, what he had seen. Something maybe the diver didn't even remember now but could dredge up. Anything.

"You can't come in here! Oh, it's you, Commander." The dour nurse on the desk that blocked the corridor did not smile.

"How is Marave?"

"If you mean the Kwajaleini patient, I'm glad to say he was much better this afternoon. He came out of the delirium. Now he is resting comfortably."

"Can he talk? Can he remember?"

"I wouldn't know, Commander. Medically he's much improved, essentially out of danger. How his mind is isn't my job."

The refuge of the mediocre, their job. If it wasn't in the job description, it didn't exist. Carter walked past her and nodded to the sleepy guard outside Marave's door. The guard waved an idle hand by way of a salute. Carter went into the room. It was quiet and dim, a single lamp on near the bed, the night now dark over the sea outside the open windows.

The diver lay as silent as he had earlier, but his hands were crossed quietly on his chest now. Relaxed. Even limp. His eyes staring up. . . .

Carter ran to the bed.

Marave lay on his back, eyes open but seeing nothing at all. A pool of blood soaked the hospital sheets from his gaping throat.

The diver's head had been almost cut off, the blood still wet and hot.

NINE

The blood was still hot.

Wilhelmina was in Carter's hand.

His eyes searched the whole room, dim with the single light in the now dark night. The room was empty. Carter crossed quickly to the open window with its curtains blowing in the soft Pacific breeze.

Shadowy shapes moved among the palms.

Figures all in black like part of the night.

Carter climbed out of the window, dropped to the ground, and ran swiftly and silently after the retreating shapes.

They moved in military precision toward one of the nine-hole golf courses. Twelve of them, by Carter's count as he followed like a phantom in pursuit: two as rear guard, two on point, two on each flank, and four in the center. They were like a patrol in enemy territory: a commando raid that had done its work and was withdrawing in good order.

Some car headlights swept the night. In the houses people played music behind lighted windows. There was a party at the golf club, shadows dancing through the wide French doors.

The retreating patrol hurried on, alert and silent,

picking its way carefully to avoid any contact, and so moving not quite as fast as it could have.

Just as the patrol reached the golf course and started to cross, moving faster now that the danger of meeting anyone was less, Carter caught up.

It was an experienced patrol, trained men. The two rear guards were close enough so that one could not be attacked without the other knowing it, yet separated just far enough that no one could attack them together.

No one except the Killmaster.

Silently he shadowed the two men across the dark night of the golf course. Under palms and through thickets of imported hibiscus and oleander. Around bunkers white in the night. Across the slick, well-watered greens. He came to a maintenance shed in a grove of palms, and for an instant the rear guards were hidden from the main body and the flank guards. Carter approached them as they passed between the small building and the palms.

Hugo leaped into Carter's hand, and he was on them. The stiletto went in under the ribs of the man on the right as Carter's arm clamped around the windpipe of the man on the left. He flung the dead man off the narrow blade, killed the second man with another single thrust, dropped his body, and was gone in the night toward the two on the right flank.

The two on the right flank were trotting single file, both watching out into the night away from the center, one looking front and side, the other back and side. Neither was looking toward the center from where Carter thrust Hugo into the rear man, left him dead, and leaped toward the front man.

The man turned. He saw Carter and raised a small, stubby submachine gun. Carter had to shoot. A single shot from Wilhelmina dropped the man.

Carter fell with the dead invader.

The burst of automatic fire came from the left. Eight guns. Bullets slammed into the dead man, whined overhead, kicked up dirt like divots from the grass of the golf course.

"Count off!" said a voice—in Japanese.

Seven voices counted. The single voice called again.

"Miko? Fortune? Shaw? Yukio?"

A silence. Then a different voice.

"They got them! All four of them."

Another silence. And still another voice.

"There's no one out there. No cover. I can see two bodies, that's all. If there's anyone close, he's behind one of the bodies. Just one man."

Carter slipped his small infrared night binoculars from his pocket and looped the cord over his ears. He could see two of them close to the ground. One had large infrared field glasses, and he was reporting what he could see. The other was also flat on the ground, but his head was raised and he looked like the leader.

Carter swept the night beyond the pair on the ground. The other six were in a bunker just to the right of the two in the open. As he watched, the two crawled back to the bunker and tumbled in. They would talk it over for a time.

Carter examined the body of the dead man that hid him. The man wore a skintight black wet suit. It was a seamless, one-piece suit, with feet and gloves, that zipped up the back with a watertight zipper. Even the face mask was built in, and it had some special device to prevent fogging. There was no way water could get in. And there was no air tank.

The dead man had been armed with the same stubby submachine gun—a 9mm PM-63 Polish-made machine pistol. It had the regular field twenty-five-round magazine. Carter stuck it into his belt.

Somewhere in the distance he heard a siren. Someone had heard the firing, and the military police were coming. Across the night in the bunker they heard it too. The moon was coming up, and the bunker would soon be more visible. They emerged from the bunker in a tight group, two walking backward to watch the rear, and the eight men in black hurried away across the golf course again.

Escape was more important to them than getting their attacker, which, to Carter, meant they had a report to make and were under orders not to be captured.

He wanted at least one of them alive.

In their tight group they headed away toward the ocean. Carter circled to get in front of them. They were moving as fast as they could while ready to defend against an attack from all sides, but he caught them at the far edge of the golf course just above the ocean-side beach. He had to separate them, split off one he could capture.

He fired a burst from his borrowed PM-63.

Two screamed in the night and went down, dead before they hit the grass.

The other six returned a fusillade that pinned him down, and Carter took cover behind trees in the now bright moonlight. Even without his infrared binoculars, Carter saw that five were bunched behind trees in a grove to his right just above the beach; the sixth was at least fifty feet away from them, alone behind a large palm farther inland. The light wind was blowing toward the sea.

Carter pulled Pierre from its place high on his thigh and hurled the deadly gas bomb to explode directly in the center of the group of five. He heard its lethal hiss, then circled quickly left and upwind to come up behind the solitary remaining invader. He slipped down his infrared binoculars, spotted the isolated man behind his large palm, and ran in a crouch to get him.

Then a violent barrage of automatic fire came from the grove where Pierre had exploded.

Carter dived frantically for the ground, rolled, crawled, and slid into a shallow fairway bunker.

His left arm burned with pain. He'd been hit in the fleshy part of his upper arm. Cursing, he stopped the blood with pressure, and peered over the edge of the bunker, his infrared binoculars still on. His quarry was running from behind the palm to rejoin the others, all alive, in the grove.

Pierre should have killed all five in seconds. There was only one answer: the special watertight wet suits were airtight too. They were as good as permanent gas masks as long as the face masks were on.

Carter took out one of the special plastic bandages he always carried, bound his arm, and prepared to crawl out of the narrow bunker. He'd have to pick them off one by one, and take the last survivor alive.

As he started to slip into the night, the six men suddenly ran out of the trees and down across the beach. Carter jumped up in pursuit. They had reached the edge of the water and were clambering into two rubber boats. Down on one knee, Carter aimed the Polish PM-63.

A glaring spotlight caught him in its brilliance, and a heavy machine gun opened fire.

Sand kicked up five feet in front of Carter.

The Killmaster dived back into the bunker.

The heavy machine gun continued to chatter as the spotlight probed slowly back and forth, up and down in search of him.

Out on the sea in the moonlight the black submersible heaved on the swells, the light on its conning tower, the machine gun behind it. The six invaders were halfway to it now in their rubber boats. Helpless, Carter watched them reach the black craft, climb aboard, and vanish below.

Men were running across the golf course behind him, but it was too late. Even as he watched, the submarine sank out of sight and was gone.

"You! Hold it right there!"

Behind him, five MPs had their weapons trained on him. Carter sighed, dropped the little PM-63, and raised his hands. The MPs moved up cautiously. The sergeant saw him.

"Oh. Sorry, sir. We had a report of automatic weapons fire."

"You heard right, Sergeant," Carter said. "A patrol of frogmen. They just made it home to their sub. I got six of them. You'll find their bodies on the golf course. You'd better have your men pick them up."

The sergeant swallowed. "Er, yes, sir."

"Now drive me back to the hospital."

"Yes, sir."

At the hospital he jumped from the Jeep. General Scott stood in front of the hospital with Major Hammond. Both were armed, pistols in holsters.

"We heard firing," the general said quietly.

"The nurse reported you went into Marave's room," Major Hammond said. "She heard a noise and went in to check and found Marave dead. She thinks you killed him, then escaped through the open window."

"We knew better," General Scott said. "Who were they? What happened?"

Carter told them about the murder of the one surviving victim of the diving off Ebaye, the squad of frogmen in their watertight, airtight, tankless wet suits, and the submersible that came to gather them in.

"None of the six you shot are alive?" the general asked.

"No."

"We finally found some Soviet survivors out there," Major Hammond said. "Two. Pure luck. They were divers in full wet suits ready to go down from a rubber boat maybe a hundred yards away from the ship. The explosion stunned both of them, but they revived drifting farther out. We missed them the first few passes."

"What did they tell you?"

"Almost nothing," General Scott said. "The ship exploded and sank within minutes, perhaps seconds. There was the explosion, great clouds of flame and smoke, and the ship was gone. They think it was some kind of torpedo."

"It wasn't the seaweed," Major Hammond said. "Not this time."

"There was no chance for anyone aboard," the

general said. "I'm sure whoever sank them counted on no survivors at all. It was just the purest chance the two survived."

"At least whoever is behind this is human—they missed the two on the raft," Major Hammond said.

"Human and perhaps Japanese," Carter said. "The raiders who killed Marave spoke in Japanese. Some of the names the commander called out were Japanese, and some weren't. It was a mixed group."

"An antiwar group gone completely insane?" General Scott wondered.

"It's possible, General," Carter agreed. "What about the laboratory tests?"

"Let's go and find out," General Scott said.

The brisk little general led the way along the hospital corridors to the laboratory. The same team—technicians, chief, and doctor—were still working on the samples of weed and water inside the glove boxes.

"We have isolated what appears to be an unknown substance in the water samples," the doctor reported to the general, "but we have no identification on it. As near as we can tell, it fits no known chemical grouping."

"How can that be, Doctor?" Carter asked. "I thought all possible structures had been worked out."

"They have, with the basic laws of chemistry we know. This compound is not possible from what I know, so I'm sending it to Washington for complete analysis."

"And the plants?" Carter asked a technician.

"Definitely a mutant of seaweeds being grown experimentally in Japan for food. We're in touch with Tokyo now to see if they have any record of this mutant."

"What have the pathologists found?"

The general answered. "They reported an hour ago, and went back to Pearl. All the victims died of nerve poisoning—an extremely potent nerve poison of some kind. They could not identify it, and two of them are world experts on poisons. In fact they took tissue samples with them to work on in Pearl and to send to every other pathologist and toxicologist in the country.''

Carter nodded. ''Can I use the radio room, General?''

''Of course, Commander. If you want me, I'll be in my office or at home. Contact me anywhere.''

Major Hammond followed the general out, and the lab team went back to work on the challenge of their unknown problem. Carter left them working, and walked through the bright moonlit night to the headquarters building. It was humming with activity as the staff communicated with the Soviet cruiser now lying offshore near where their electronic surveillance ship had gone down. The big question was whether or not to allow the Soviet crew shore leave on Kwajalein. They were involving Moscow and Washington in the decision.

Carter found a guard on the radio room door; the room itself was deserted. He sat at the microphone, gave the code numbers, and waited for the dulcet tones of the computer.

''Hello, N3, what can I give you tonight?'' the voice purred.

''A little time with the chief, if you please.''

''Well, we'll just see if that can be arranged.''

Hawk came on almost before the computer had stopped purring at Carter. ''Anything, N3?''

''I think so,'' Carter said, and he described all the events of the day and evening. ''Now we know the submersible is behind it all, including the weed, and someone is behind the submersible. Whoever it is didn't want Marave to talk about what he'd seen, which means there was something to see. The seaweed isn't a natural event.''

''No,'' Hawk said, worry etched in his voice. ''They spoke Japanese?''

''And the plant seems to have a connection to Japan.''

"They're pretty advanced in underwater research."

"Even to breathing without air tanks underwater?"

Carter listened to Hawk puffing on his cigar. "A wet suit protects?"

"As long as it's watertight."

Hawk went on puffing. "What I don't get is what anyone stands to gain out of this. What's the purpose?"

"Blackmail? Get the world powers to stop doing something under threat of turning the plant loose in vital waterways?"

"The peace movement?"

"General Scott sees it as a possibility."

"General Scott was sure it was the Russians," Hawk said drily. "What else can you do there, Nick?"

"Nothing," Carter said. "What did you learn about that cove in New Guinea?"

"Nothing," Hawk said. "You'd better get over there."

"Any other reports of the weed?"

"Not yet. Tomorrow morning, take a navy VTOL. I'll have one on Kwajalein by dawn."

"We'd better have something else here fast," Carter said.

"What's that?"

"Something to stop the weed."

Hawk puffed on the cigar in his distant office.

TEN

The pilot of the British Navy Harrier pointed down to the dense jungle of the coast of New Guinea. Carter looked at the endless green, the almost hidden rivers, the numberless coves, and the cloud-wreathed mountains towering ahead in the distance. Even today, in remote mountain valleys and dense jungle depths far from the coast or the main rivers, there were people living in the Stone Age.

"That's the mouth of the Sepik up there, Commander," the pilot's voice said over the intercom. "With the Aussie's directions, I'll set you down in that district commissioner's lap."

The broad mouth of the large river was clearly visible farther up the coast. The Harrier jet went down rapidly, sweeping in low over the coast and a small cove at which Carter stared. Even from the jet he could see the dark, almost black color of the water, the shoots protruding like snake heads above the surface, the dead fish and small animals.

"Swing back out to sea for a moment, Lieutenant," Carter instructed.

"It's your joyride," the cheerful young pilot said.

The Harrier circled over the ocean again, and Carter

saw the shadow spreading out from the cove that indicated the growing weed. It was already some fifty
miles off the coast at the point of the arc, fifty miles
along the coast in either direction. Dead fish and even
large animals dotted the silent, ominous surface of the
dark sea.

"Let's find the village," Carter said.

"Righto."

The Harrier swept up and over and down again across
the coast and circled a small village less than a quarter
of a mile from the weed-choked cove. In the center of
the village was a large thatched building of palm fronds
and bamboo. The Harrier pilot grinned, pointed down,
and settled the jet lower until it hovered directly over the
open space in front of the large building, then slowly
settled to a gentle landing.

"Piece of cake," the young pilot said.

"Nice job," Carter complimented him as he climbed
out.

The pilot grinned from the cockpit but didn't get out.
"Always glad to oblige a friendly navy. Sorry I can't
stay." He glanced around the silent village. "Lively-
looking town. But duty calls."

Carter did a slow three-sixty. There was no sign of
life. "You have to leave?"

"Orders, you know. Deliver and split, that was the in-
struction. See you, Yank."

He waved, brought up the power, and the Harrier
rose into the air in its vertical takeoff and was gone over
the trees that grew thickly around the village.

Carter picked up his sea bag and again looked slowly
all around him. The village seemed to consist of twenty
or twenty-five neat grass huts, clean and well made.
They were on high ground cleared from the jungle, the
bare dirt packed hard by generations and swept clean,
the jungle itself only feet from the last house.

There were cooking areas in front of each hut, pots
over the fires, dogs skulking warily around the buildings.

But no sign of people.

Carter picked up his bag and walked slowly around the village looking at all the huts. Everything seemed to be there inside the huts: sleeping mats, weapons, utensils, masks, ceremonial robes. Cooking pots hung over all the fires, most still full of food. But the fires were out, the food cold. Eating bowls sat on the ground, some with food still in them, as if the eaters had simply dropped them and run.

He crossed the open area of cement-hard dirt between the first row of huts and the large bamboo and palm thatch house. It was the standard white-man's house in a native village. One story, a low, shaded veranda around three sides, windows on the inner wall of the veranda closed not with glass but with mosquito netting and bamboo blinds. The deserted veranda creaked under his footsteps. The door was unlocked. He put down his bag, drew Wilhelmina, and pushed the door open. Nothing moved inside.

Carter slipped in like a shadow, flattened himself against the wall, and swiftly surveyed the room. It was one large living room with old and dusty bamboo and rattan furniture and a bar that opened into the kitchen at the rear. It was neat and yet disordered, things in piles. The room of a man who lived alone and had for some time. The doors to two bedrooms to the right were open, a large, four-poster bed with mosquito netting in one, the other, cluttered with old furniture and junk, being used as a storeroom.

He crossed to the kitchen. The table in the living room near the kitchen was set for breakfast, napkin unfolded at one place. In the kitchen itself, eggs were cold in the pan, toast dry and hard on the counter, a glass of milk warm and curdled.

Carter returned Wilhelmina to her holster and went back into the living room. The same story as outside in the village. In the middle of breakfast, or about to start, everyone had vanished. To where? And why? He searched the large house without finding a single clue.

He left his bag in the house and went outside again. In the shadows of the veranda he slowly surveyed the entire silent village. The dogs, grown bolder now that he was out of sight, nosed through the abandoned cook pots and bowls, but there was no sign of human life. It was as if time had stopped in the village, the people vanished into another dimension, another time warp.

He saw the movement far to the left.

A tiny, almost invisible movement of the jungle wall that ringed the village.

It came again.

Carter showed no reaction, made no move to reveal he had seen anything. But he had seen all he needed.

Someone was out there at the edge of the jungle watching him.

It was the smallest motion of the thick foliage, but Carter's trained gaze had detected the glisten of an eye, a fleeting image of black skin where a hand or perhaps a finger moved the green.

He walked down the steps of the house and turned away from the movement in the jungle. He began to search the huts one by one, working his way around toward where the movement had been. Halfway there, he went into a hut that backed against the jungle.

Inside the dim hut, Hugo leaped into his hand from his sleeve, and he quickly cut a hole in the rear wall, slipped through, and went into the jungle.

In the thick vegetation, among the green, sun-dappled leaves of the jungle with its heavy green roof above, the Killmaster circled as silently as any jungle cat to come up behind where he had seen the faint movement, the flash of skin and eye. His eyes slowly grew accustomed to the dim green light, and he sensed he was close to where he had seen the movement. Crouched low against the massive trunk of a tree covered with lichens and fungus, he waited and watched.

The endless sound and movement of the timeless sun-filtered jungle, unchanged for millions of years.

Slow time.

Almost without time.

The shape seemed to grow out of the shadows themselves. Then another. And another.

Carter saw three thickset, naked men moving so silently they seemed to float on the thick jungle air, part of the shadowed light, an illusion.

But they were very real, and if they made no sound, they did leave a trail as they passed Carter from the direction of the village moving away and deeper into the jungle. But they were out of sight almost as soon as they had passed, the bent leaves and springing-back ferns the only sign of their passage. It was enough.

Carter followed them, more silent than they were, the shadow of shadows.

He was never close enough to see them, or even hear them, but he was led on by the almost invisible trail that was as good as a six-lane highway to a trained tracker.

He was led away from the village and the coast toward the far-off mountains but not near the mountains, led no more than a mile inland from the village to a tinier settlement of huts. A few other men and women noisily greeted the newcomers in a language Carter didn't know. The three men spoke quickly and excitedly, gesturing back toward the village. Carter had found his missing villagers. Or some of them.

He stepped out of the jungle shadows, Wilhelmina pointed straight at the three men. Some of the women saw him first, and they screamed and scattered.

The three men did not run. They knew who he was, or at least they knew what he wanted.

"What happened?"

He watched them, looking slowly from one to the other. The oldest stepped forward.

"They come. We run away. We hear plane. We go see. We see you. We not know what you are, so we go away."

"What happened before I got here? What happened after you found the weed in the cove?"

Two of them looked as if they'd just as soon run right

then, Wilhelmina or no Wilhelmina. The older spokes-
man trembled, but he stood his ground.

"You sit. We tell. Okay, boss?"

The old man indicated a comfortable patch of dirt in
the shade of a hut and some trees, and he offered a chew
of lime and betel nut on a leaf. His English was much
better and a lot more colloquial and even Americanized
than the usual Pisin-speaking Papuan. There was at
least one long trip far from New Guinea in his history.
Carter refused the betel nut, but he walked to the
meeting place and sat on the ground.

"Where did you travel to?" he asked the old man as
the three sat down and began to chew on their betel nuts
and lime. The other two were immediately happier.

"Me go on ship many time. Then go on big plane. Go
London. Go San Francisco. Me learn cook Australia,
go many place. You American?"

"American," Carter said. "What happened after the
cove?"

The old man looked solemn and shook his head. The
other two went on chewing and keeping an eye on their
escape route. In the jungle all around, Carter sensed the
others watching and waiting.

"Fish die, animal die. Weed very bad," the old man
said. "Old boss he tell us go away from water, come
back village. He make report Moresby, tell them weed
in cove and fish all dead. Then we all go eat. Go hut and
talk. Then they come."

"They?"

One of the others was getting up some courage.
Maybe it was the betel nut. "Many fella come along
me!"

"A lot of men?" Carter asked.

The old man nodded, his eyes still scared. "They
come, we run. I hide. I see."

"See what?"

"Many men. Come cove way. All black but not black
men, yes? Have water clothes, guns, catch people, catch
boss in house. Take away. We see, we run, they no

catch. We go behind, see cove, they go in! Not die. Great black fish come from water, have light, eyes like house. Many men go into big fish, it swim away, sink. All gone.''

The submersible. Or one just like it. To Carter it sounded like some kind of mistake in the cove, the experiment more successful than they had expected, or maybe they had not known an Australian was in the area with contact to Port Moresby. If so, they had been too late. Carter wondered if they knew that, whoever they were.

''You can go back to the village,'' he told the three men. ''I don't think they'll be back, and there's no danger.''

The three nodded sadly.

''All gone. People.''

''You three are the only survivors?''

The three men nodded.

''We go back, look, wait, maybe people come back,'' the older one said, but his voice showed that he did not believe it. His people were gone forever.

Carter wished he could have told him he was wrong, but he couldn't. He didn't think the villagers or the old commissioner would be back. Whoever was behind the weed and the submersible did not like witnesses.

''What will you do?'' he asked gently.

''We live here, have new village.''

''We watch old village. Wait.''

''Many fella belong us come back.''

The other two had more hope. They had less experience, less imagination. Maybe that was better.

Carter left the three of them standing in the tiny village and started back for the empty settlement. Behind him he heard the other people slowly emerging from the jungle. They would vanish at the slightest sound, the appearance of any stranger, for a long time.

When he reached the deserted village with its larger house, he didn't stop, but went on all the way back to the cove. In the hardened mud at the edge he found the faint tracks of feet with swim fins that showed where the wet-suited attackers had returned to the water.

He backtracked slowly to the village itself, searching every inch of ground for any evidence of who and what the attackers were. He found nothing.

In the village he went back up the steps of the kidnapped commissioner's house and searched the veranda. Nothing.

Inside he searched the living room. Nothing.

The bedroom with its mosquito-net-draped fourposter yielded no clues.

In the storeroom he surveyed the clutter.

And heard the soft sound behind him. Out in the big main room. Pressed against the wall he peered out.

A figure in a black wet suit stood in the room.

Hugo jumped into Carter's hand. The figure had its back to him. He leaped toward it and reached around to clamp his arm around its throat.

And was hurled through the air to crash against the wall as the black figure attacked.

ELEVEN

Carter bounded away from the wall and Hugo slashed at the silent intruder.

The attacker kicked the stiletto into the air with a swift karate kick that numbed Carter's hand.

Carter let fly a quick kick into the attacker's ribs that should have broken bones.

The figure in the black wet suit and mask twisted with the force of the kick into a somersault. The unknown assailant came up breathing hard but uninjured.

Carter moved in with a kick to the chin that missed.

The attacker chopped for Carter's neck.

The Killmaster twisted under the blow, came up inside the lethal hands, grappled close. . . .

And looked into the laughing eyes behind the mask, then felt the soft breasts hidden under the wet suit, the slender body tight against him.

"I wondered how good your training was," Siobhan O'Neill said. "You're not just a DOD Intelligence officer."

"And you're not just Aussie Naval Intelligence," Carter said, still holding her close against him. "I would have killed most agents with the first kick."

"It was good, best I've been up against," she said,

taking off her mask and kissing him. "You want to talk more shop, or shall we try that bed in there?"

He picked her up lightly. "A four-poster and mosquito netting. How could anyone resist."

She was unbuttoning his shirt before they got to the bed. He pulled back the heavy mosquito netting and put her on the bed. She had his boots and pants off. He pulled the wet suit bottom down. She was naked under the suit. She dug her hands into his shorts and pulled them off. He had her wet suit top off, her breasts falling free and loose, the nipples hard. She buried her face in his neck, moving warm and soft and hard against him.

He closed the mosquito netting and stroked the length of her body as her mouth worked hot and wet against his throat. Under the thick netting the light was an ancient yellow, distant, filtered through ages of dust and colonial memories.

Under her, deep in the soft mattress, the thick muted sound and light of the mosquito netting. Hot light and hot sound. Breathing hot, close. Heavy warmth and seeking mouth, urgent, all over him. Breathing and searching each other under the yellow light of the dusty bamboo room. Only an empty village beyond the close enclosing heat of the netting that was in another world. A world of two bodies entwined like one animal seeking itself.

They breathed hard. Lay side by side. Unmoving. Only breathing and looking up at the yellow canopy of muted light. Isolated under the netting and in themselves. They lay and touched and did not move, only breathed. Breathed hard and lay close but not moving until they could stand it no longer and he rose up on his arms and she opened her legs as wide as the bed to draw him into her.

The passion seemed to be held in, enclosed by the mosquito netting, enclosed in the ancient yellow light, encapsulated in a thick liquid light and silence that flowed all around them as he searched inside her, probed deeper and deeper, and she drew him in, held him tight inside her, locked him in as hot and close as the yellow light and the thick netting itself.

Cries echoed from the yellow light, echoed from the bamboo walls and palm roof, throbbed through the village and the jungle and the far-off cove where the dead fish and the dead animals floated. They were cries of live animals entwined and slippery and hot and panting and breathing . . . breathing . . .

The yellow light seemed to come from nowhere. Carter lay on his back and looked at the thatched roof above him, the heat washing over him as if he were in some kind of steam bath. He had the sensation that he had been on a trip. Somewhere out of time. As if time had stopped and he had returned to another world.

"Nice," Siobhan said.

She smiled where she lay beside him in the big four-poster bed under the thick mosquito netting with the hot tropical sun outside. Her slim, strong hand played on his belly, stroked his legs.

"Better," he said. "Why?"

"Orders," she said. "Same as you, N3."

"You've been doing some homework."

"We're not all kangaroos and wallabies, Nick. It so happens we've got a man who once worked with your boss."

"Everyone worked with my boss," Carter said with a sigh.

"No, only the best in all the services."

"Including the KGB."

"We can be a pretty small club sometimes."

"Like now," Carter said. "What are your orders, Siobhan?"

"Find out what's behind the weed and the submarine."

"Why come here?"

"It's the first reported occurrence. Or first definite reported occurrence."

"First? You know others besides Kwajalein?"

She rolled close against him, her mouth breathing on his throat.

"There are three other coves in New Guinea where the weed is growing. They happened after this one, and there was no old commissioner to report them right away. Word drifted in over the last week."

"And definite?"

"When we ran a computer scan we came up with a year-old report from one of our stringers in Japan. There was something like the fast-growing weed reported from a remote area of Japan, but it seems to have made no ripples."

"Coverup?"

"Possible. We checked back with our man yesterday. He can't find any coverup, but there's no record of anything being done beyond the initial report, either."

"It just lay there?"

"So it seems."

Carter was thoughtful. "There seems to be a strong Japanese flavor to the whole thing."

"But no definite lead."

Carter nodded, then turned to look at her naked body. In the yellow light under the netting, she looked like a soft vision from some great painting. She ran her fingers lightly along his chest and belly, and smiled at him.

"We have to find a lead," he said.

"Yes, we do."

"We should start looking."

"Yes, we should."

"Now."

"Even sooner."

Her mouth was soft and wet on his throat. His hand touched her where she was soft and wet.

"Work is important."

"Very."

"We have to search the village."

"All of it."

"It won't go away."

"No."

"We have time."

"All there is."

"We could do something else, and this house, the village, will still be here."

"We certainly could."

And they did.

Some hours later, dressed now in almost identical camouflage coveralls, they slipped out of the bamboo and palm thatch commissioner's house and spread out to search the village. A low, cooling evening sunlight slanted through the silent village. Faces peered at them from the jungle wall, but the natives did not return. Not as long as they moved among the neat huts, their presence unexplained and mysterious to the villagers.

They found nothing at all in the clean, swept huts.

In the commissioner's house once more, they each searched opposite sides of the main room. They moved methodically, the tedious work as much a part of an agent's expertise as slipping across heavily guarded borders or killing. Outside in the fading evening light the people were coming into the village. They came warily, testing each step as if the ground were quicksand. Life had not taught them to feel secure with light-skinned strangers.

Siobhan tried the kitchen; Carter went into the cluttered storeroom. It took him so long to plow through the mess of stored furniture, old suitcases, and rusted filing cabinets that Siobhan came to help him.

"Nothing that adds up to anything in the kitchen," she reported, beginning to turn over the stacked furniture and pull out its stuffing.

"I haven't hit a bonanza," Carter said.

They tore apart what was left of the room and came up empty-handed. There was only the bedroom left.

"This is for something other than searching," Carter said.

"Ready when you are, N3."

Carter laughed. "Duty first, Commander."

But there was nothing in the bedroom that could be remotely connected to the silent invaders or Japan or the weed or a submarine.

"What now?" Siobhan asked.

Carter looked around the cluttered house. It was something out of the last century, and more than time had passed it by. A different world had swallowed its owner.

"Where are these other coves?" he said.

"Do you think we'll do any better there?"

"We couldn't do worse. We have to get a lead somewhere."

"If there is one," Siobhan said. "These people are pretty damned careful."

"Can you get us a ride?"

"Of course." She smiled. "Tomorrow morning soon enough?"

"Is that the best you can do?"

"No, but I think I can stall that long."

He grinned. "Do your worst."

She went out into the dusk of the slowly reviving village. Fires burned now in front of some of the huts, the bolder villagers watching Siobhan with only a little wariness. Her transmitter was in her backpack. As she took it out and set it up to call her headquarters, the native who had traveled to London and San Francisco, the boldest of all of them, came across the hard-packed open area in front of the commissioner's house. He looked at Carter, then nodded to Siobhan O'Neill.

"You smart fella, boss. You bring woman."

"Commander O'Neill is from the Royal Australian Navy," Carter said. "She is here working to find out about those attackers too."

A female Australian military officer in his village was a little too much even for such a world traveler. He shifted his feet as if he didn't know whether to salute or run. He licked his lips and grinned. Siobhan continued setting up. Carter noticed he had something in his hand.

"You have something you want to show me? What's your name?"

"Name Tukum along me."

"My name is Carter, Tukum. Is what you have in your hand for me?"

"Car-ter!" The native, Tukum, beamed.

Carter pointed to his hand. "What do you have there?"

Tukum looked down at his hand. Then he nodded, opened his hand, and showed it to Carter. A ballpoint pen lay in his rough hand. A white pen that looked expensive. Carter took it.

"Me find by water. Where we see black not black men take boss to boat that sink."

Carter looked at the pen. It was sleek and expensive in white enamel trimmed with gold. Gold lettering on the barrel read Takeda Research Ltd.

"Siobhan!"

He showed her the pen. She looked at it, then looked up at him.

"A Japanese company. They're big in sea farming and underwater research." Siobhan watched him. "You want me to tell my people to pick us up right now?"

Carter smiled. "What's one day?"

"What indeed."

"We have to eat. There's a table all set inside the house."

"I've got some fine emergency rations."

"A feast," he said. "And later we can plan our course of action. It might take all night."

She turned to her transmitter. "Pick me up tomorrow morning at dawn. We'll have a passenger. Commander Carter of the U.S. Navy. Over and out."

They smiled at each other. Carter took his survival knife from his pack and gave it to Tukum. The native beamed as Carter and Siobhan went back into the house where the table was still set and waiting. They let it wait.

TWELVE

The Australian Navy helicopter took them down the coast to Lae where the Australian Air Force twin-jet high-altitude night fighter waited to take them on. The pilot wasn't happy to see them.

"Bloody pain in the arse. Joyriders!"

He was a skinny, sallow man with a narrow face and bloated features who was ten years too old for his rank and looked as if he'd spent his life inside a pub. Which was probably why he was ten years too old for his rank.

"We'll buy the beer in Japan," Carter said.

The pilot reddened. "Screw you, mate."

"That," Carter said, "you'll have to take care of yourself. Shall we get aboard?"

"When I jolly well say to get aboard," the pilot snapped.

"No," Siobhan said icily, "when *I* say to get aboard, Lieutenant! And I say we board *now*!"

The surly pilot glared at her. "Copilot ain't here yet."

"Then get him!"

The sullen pilot went on glaring at her, but he also went to find the copilot.

"Let's get our gear," Siobhan said.

They picked up their flight suits and parachutes at the air force depot on the field, then returned to the waiting jet. The pilot and a very young, scared-looking lieutenant were waiting in their flight gear, small submachine guns hooked to survival harnesses.

"You got a flight plan I can file?" the pilot said.

Siobhan handed him her orders. "Tokyo, I think, Lieutenant. If you can stay sober that long."

"Ah, go—"

Carter didn't hear whatever the overage lieutenant said after that. His peripheral vision caught an unmarked assault helicopter landing not a hundred yards away, and a faint voice on the radio inside the jet said: ". . .unauthorized landing! Identify yourself, helicopter! Come in . . ."

Six men in black jumped out of the helicopter and ran toward the night fighter jet.

"Down!" Carter yelled, Wilhelmina in his hand.

Siobhan was down even before his command was finished. So was the sallow, scrawny, overage pilot, his submachine gun already coming up in his hands. Only the young copilot blinked, and looked around to see why he should hit the ground.

The volley from the six AK-47 assault rifles cut the young copilot to pieces, his blood showering the three on the ground.

Carter dropped two of the attackers with single shots through their foreheads at fifty yards, the backs of their heads bursting open in halos of blood.

Siobhan got two more with a burst of her Uzi, blowing out their bellies in gouts of red against the black cloth.

The surly pilot mowed down the last two with his submachine gun, breaking their legs. They flopped screaming on the runway like dying fish in pools of their own blood.

"Over there!" Carter cried.

The scrawny pilot reacted even faster than Siobhan. He may have been a foul-mouthed, insubordinate, generally nasty drunk, but he was a good soldier. He sprayed the four black-garbed attackers running in from the left where they had circled unseen while their six comrades attacked straight on. Two went down gushing blood and pieces of flesh and bone, the others hit the ground and returned fire. The pilot was hit.

"Shit!" The pilot rolled behind a jet wheel, blood running down his left arm.

Siobhan pinned down the two attackers with short bursts from the Uzi.

Carter was busy with the four that came from the right in the cover of a row of parked trucks. There was no way he could get a clear shot at them, no time to try to take them on the flank, and it had all happened and was happening so fast there was no help coming.

He pulled Pierre from between his legs under his fatigues. These attackers were not in wet suits and masks. He waited until they were bunched behind the nearest truck, then arched the gas bomb unerringly over the truck to explode inches behind them.

Only one had time to scream before he died in the lethal fumes.

The two Siobhan had pinned down made their break when she ran out of ammunition. While she changed clips, they ran for their helicopter, pausing only long enough to kill the two wounded men still writhing on the ground with single shots to the head. They reached their chopper, which lifted off immediately, swung rapidly away north toward the ocean low across the field, and was gone.

The wounded pilot stood up holding his bloody arm. "Get in! We'll shoot the bastards down!"

Carter and Siobhan jumped up and started to climb into the night fighter. At that moment the air base security forces arrived in a scream of sirens, and a horde of armed MPs poured out of various vehicles. They quickly surrounded the night fighter and its three defenders, weapons aimed. A tall major strode out toward Carter, Siobhan, and the wounded pilot.

"Christ," the pilot muttered, "*now* they show up! Bloody useless!"

"Drop your weapons and remain where you are!" the major commanded.

"Strewth!" the pilot snarled. "We're off to catch the bloody villains, you idiot!"

"Drop those weapons and put your hands up!" the major repeated.

Siobhan stepped forward. "I'm Commander O'Neill, Naval Intelligence on a top-priority mission. We must take off at once and try to catch that helicopter, Major."

"I'll count to three," the major barked, "then we open fire."

"Major—!" Siobhan began.

"One . . ."

Carter sighed. "Put the weapons down, troops. Some people can't think beyond the tip of their nose."

The major reddened. "Two . . ."

"Sorry," Siobhan apologized, and put down her Uzi. "All armies have them."

Carter laid Wilhelmina on the runway. The scrawny pilot tossed his submachine gun into the air in disgust, letting it crash behind him.

"We got a dead Aussie here," the pilot said. "Maybe you got time to pick him up . . . sir."

"I see thirteen bodies, and anyone can wear an Australian uniform. We'll just see who you three are at headquarters! Take them in!"

"Think you'll get a bloody medal, don't you?" the pilot snarled. "Bloody post in the Antarctic, that's what you'll get when these two VIPs here are through with you, chum."

The major reddened again with anger, but his eyes flickered nervously for the first time. "All right, march!"

They were marched to a personnel carrier, herded in, and driven off across the base to the security forces headquarters. There they were ordered out of the carrier and marched into the commandant's office under full guard, the officious major watching them with his gun drawn. He made his report of the shooting fray.

"Four of these unidentified persons in a large and dangerous firefight with fourteen others, sir. Two of the survivors escaped in the unidentified helicopter. One of this lot—wearing an air force flight outfit—was killed. Following standard operating procedure, I disarmed and arrested these three and brought them in for interrogation."

The major finished, stepped back smartly, and saluted. The commandant, a colonel, nodded.

"Thank you, Major. Well done." He looked sternly at Carter, Siobhan, and the pilot. Then he blinked, and looked at the pilot again.

"Davies?"

"I ain't bloody Genghis Khan, Colonel."

The colonel looked at the major, then back at the pilot. "Can you explain what you are doing with these people, Lieutenant Davies?"

"I can, sir," Siobhan said. "Commander Siobhan O'Neill, Naval Intelligence, on special detached assignment by direct order of the War Office."

The colonel blinked even more, looked toward the major again, then back at Siobhan, his mouth open but no sound coming out.

Siobhan succinctly explained the entire firefight, finishing with, "So we were about to pursue the chopper, Colonel, with a good chance of overtaking it, when your major there surrounded us, somewhat after the horse had left the barn, and wouldn't listen to Lieutenant Davies, or to me even when I identified myself. I'm afraid Canberra is going to be a little annoyed at the stupid interference with a top-secret, urgent combined operation between us and the United States."

The major was stubborn. "Standard operating procedure, sir. Unexplained armed action by unauthorized personnel on air force property: arrest all parties and bring in for immediate interrogation. How do we know that story isn't all drivel? Probably a pack of lies, if I'm any judge.''

"Well," the colonel said, "we'll just check out your story, miss. Meanwhile, we'll hold you—"

"Code: Black Jack Ballarrat, orders Lord Nelson five," Siobhan snapped.

It was the colonel's turn to go white, then red, then white again. He stared at Siobhan, swallowed hard, then spoke weakly. "One to ten."

"Seven," Siobhan said quietly.

The colonel cleared his throat, then stood up. "I . . . er, we had no way of knowing. You should have checked in and—"

"I did, Colonel. With your intelligence people. Unfortunately, the major there refused to listen to anything we had to say. I'm afraid he lost us any chance to catch those attackers—perhaps learn where they came from—and he has held up our mission by an hour or more so far. If you're finished with us now, we'd like to get back to our work. May I ask if anyone has attempted to identify the bodies of the attackers? I mean, while you've been so busy arresting our own people?"

The colonel was beet red. "Major?"

"Er, no, sir. I thought it more important—"

"Stop thinking!" the colonel roared, glaring at the officer. "Go and check those bodies for any identification! Now!"

The major almost ran out of the office.

"We have to get back to the jet and take off, Colonel," Siobhan said. "Can we have another copilot?"

"Of course. At once. I . . . I apologize for the major's stupidity. If I'd been there—"

The pilot snickered. The colonel froze in fury. It was becoming obvious why the pilot was very old for a lieutenant. Carter grinned. He was getting to like the brusque, bitter, foul-mouthed Davies.

"We'll take off in fifteen minutes. Have the major report to the jet anything he found on the bodies,"

Siobhan said. "And send a medic for Lieutenant Davies."

They left without looking at the furious colonel again. A captain loudly ordered the driver of the personnel carrier to take them back to the jet. When they arrived, Davies checked out all the undercarriage and fuselage for bullet damage but found none. While the medics treated Davies, Carter and Siobhan checked the control linkage. Nothing seemed to have been damaged. The new copilot showed up within minutes, another lieutenant almost as old as Davies.

"Not you, Perkins," Davies groaned.

"Why not? You're not the only one the colonel hates," the new copilot said. "Where are we off to?"

"Bloody Tokyo."

The new copilot, Perkins, shrugged. "Good as anywhere. I know some skirts in Tokyo."

Davies brightened. "Marvelous."

They were ready to take off when the major appeared. He had found no identification at all on the dead attackers—Carter hadn't expected he would—and reported that they had been of all different races and nationalities as far as he could tell.

"Four Japanese, three blacks, two that looked like Polynesians, the rest Caucasians of various types."

They nodded, then dismissed the major. Five minutes later the night fighter was at the end of the runway waiting for clearance to take off, and ten minutes later they were already looking back at Lae and the rapidly receding green coast of New Guinea.

The jet flew at thirty thousand feet north across the Admiralty Islands and the Carolines to Guam in the Marianas where they stopped to refuel. In the air again, they flew straight on toward Tokyo, passing directly over the dark volcanic peak of Mt. Suribachi on Iwo Jima.

"Hope your skirts are bloody ready for action, Perkins," Davies said as they came within sight of the

Japanese coast and he descended to twenty thousand feet.

The explosion tore the night fighter apart.

Carter found himself sailing high, still strapped into the ejected seat. The seat began to curve over and down, and the parachute opened.

He gasped for air in the thin atmosphere.

His oxygen mask had been torn away, and he breathed hard, but he had already fallen to fifteen thousand feet, and the air came to meet his lungs.

He floated down slowly in the early morning sky, breathing deeply, the smoking remains of the shattered jet spiraling away below.

Half a torn and shattered seat floated down to his right, the parachute open, the headless body of one of the pilots pouring blood into the high sky like a red Niagara that evaporated into empty air as it fell toward earth.

Far to the left another parachute floated down, the ejection seat dangling. An empty seat. Whose seat?

"Fucking bloody major!"

Almost on top of Carter, another ejection seat floated down on its parachute, Lieutenant Davies swearing as he swung near Carter.

"They had to've planted the bloody bomb while he was playing bloody policeman with us! Couldn't even bloody well guard a bloody jet for a bloody fucking twenty minutes!"

Then the empty seat—?

Carter stared across the distance to the empty seat dangling from its parachute.

A woman he had been with, next to, inside, only a day ago? Half a day? A woman he had been coming closer to every second. Bright, strong, trained and skilled, slim and beautiful. Gone. Never again her laugh, her smile, her hands on his body. . . .

"Get ready to unbuckle, mate," Davies called as he drifted away to the right. "We're going in the drink."

Carter looked below. The coast of Japan was directly

ahead, a populated beach area from the look of it. He could see cars and houses and even what looked like police emergency trucks heading toward where they would come down. The faint wail of sirens. But they would hit in the water, and the surf was rough. Davies was already below him and unbuckling to swim when he hit.

Carter hauled on the shrouds to slip sideways so he could hang longer in the air and work himself closer and closer to land. Below, he saw Davies hit the water. A sleek patrol boat headed out toward him with a long white wake as it tore through the water on its rescue mission. He continued sideslipping, the land coming closer, and saw ahead in an open field the canopy of another parachute. The empty seat? Another pang hit him for the loss of Siobhan, and then he was over the coast and coming down rapidly in an open, parklike area of grass just behind the beach.

He hit as softly as possible, and the Japanese rescue teams were running toward him before he could even unbuckle and stand up. A quick, efficient, polite officer led them.

"You are okay?"

"I think so," Carter said. "The pilot?"

"We picked one out of the water. Another was killed in the explosion. Do you know what happened?"

"A bomb was planted on the plane. No question."

"We have not recovered the wreckage. Why would someone wish to put a bomb on your aircraft, Mr.—?"

"Commander," Carter said, "Commander Nelson Carter, U.S. Department of Defense Intelligence. We are on an important secret investigation, and someone didn't want us to complete it."

"I see," the officer said, nodding. "Yes, that checks with the other agent's story. Perhaps you will accompany us to police headquarters. We will have someone from the Interior Ministry come from Tokyo with your ambassador to arrange all the details."

"Other agent?" Carter said.

"Commander O'Neill."

Carter blinked. "She's . . . alive?"

"I certainly hope so," Siobhan's voice said behind him.

He whirled. She was in his arms. The Japanese policemen smiled.

"How?" he said.

"I was thrown clear of the seat, fell a couple of thousand feet free-fall, then revived enough to open my emergency chute." She looked at him. "They told me one was dead. I didn't know which one."

They held each other there in the early morning Japanese sunlight.

THIRTEEN

Two polite but eagle-eyed internal security men came with the man from the Interior Ministry and the American military attaché. The American wasn't polite until Carter gave him the code words, and then he was stiff and wary. A Company man, CIA, he didn't much like competition in his territory, and he liked top-secret personnel he knew nothing about even less.

Carter explained to the two Japanese security men exactly what had happened, gave them codes to check with Washington and Canberra, told them to take good care of Davies, and instructed the military attaché to take them to the ambassador himself. The CIA man wasn't pleased, but he took them to Tokyo in the helicopter that had brought him and the Interior Ministry representative. The Japanese security people had their own chopper.

"Anything I can do, just say it," the military attaché said as they flew low toward Tokyo over the neat, populated Japanese countryside.

"We appreciate that," Siobhan said.

"If it's happening in Japan, I know it," the attaché said. "I could save you some time."

"We'll keep it in mind," Carter said.

"Just let me know what you need," the attaché said.

"We'll be sure to call on you first," Siobhan said.

"Tell me the problem," the attaché said, "what you want to know, I can put you on the fast track."

"Just be ready," Carter said. "We might call on you anytime."

"Better if I got started now. Just fill me in on the mission. I can set you up."

"It's too bad we can't," Carter said. "Probably slow it all up, but that's red tape for you, right?"

The attaché scowled and glared at them. "I've got top rating on this post, top clearance. Anything happens in my yard, I need to know."

"Too bad Washington doesn't see it that way," Carter said.

"You know how they are in Canberra," Siobhan said.

"Dammit!" the attaché said. "This is my store! You tell me what you're working on!"

Carter smiled. "Sorry. Ambassador's ears only."

"You think lousy DOD Intelligence carries weight over the Company, Carter?" the attaché fumed. "I'll have you on the rug so fast you'll be back pounding a desk in Newport News in two hours."

"I'm terrified," Carter said drily. "Why don't you call Langley right now, save time."

The attaché glared at them both, then turned his back and looked down at the outskirts of the sprawling metropolis of Tokyo. It is as modern as any city in the world, and yet the ancient castle of the Tokugawa shoguns, now the Imperial Palace, was still there as it had been when the city was known as Edo, the seat of the Tokugawa power, and the emperor had still been hidden in faraway Kyoto practicing his tea ceremony and paper folding.

The chopper settled them gently, and the ambassador himself waited to greet them. From the nervous look on the diplomat's face it was clear he had been in touch with Washington, probably with the President. The military attaché scowled even more when he saw the ambassador.

"The packages from Kwajalein and Canberra are here, Commander," the ambassador said without even waiting for a formal welcome. "We have them in the safe, untouched and unopened as instructed."

"Good," Carter said.

Ignored by everyone, the military attaché/CIA man stalked away.

"Takeda?" Siobhan said.

"You have an appointment with the managing director in two hours. I'm sure you'd like to clean up after . . . the, ah, crash. We have a fresh uniform for Commander Carter. But for Commander O'Neill . . ."

"Just some camouflage fatigues will suit me, Mr. Ambassador."

"I'd rather stay out of uniform, too, Mr. Ambassador," Carter said. "Fatigues will do me fine."

"Of course. Then come with me, we'll get you outfitted and comfortable."

In the embassy living quarters, Carter showered and dressed in the new fatigues someone had laid out on the bed of the guest bedroom. Siobhan sang in the room next door. It was tempting, but the meeting with the officials of Takeda Research Ltd. was too important. Carter sighed. Sometimes work did get in the way.

"Ready?" Siobhan stood in the doorway, the regulation-issue fatigues looking somehow like chic sportswear on her slim body.

"Ready."

She watched him. "Let's wrap this one up fast."

"Even faster."

She smiled. "Right, mate."

The ambassador was waiting for them downstairs, and they went out to his official limousine. The marine guards were very visible around the car after the attack in Lae and the bomb on the night fighter. Carter and Siobhan were under tight security. For the time being they would put up with it.

The limousine parked under the high-rise office building in downtown Tokyo. They went up in a private elevator to the executive offices of Takeda Research. A brisk secretary ushered them into a large office furnished in leather and velvet, and paneled in dark wood; it looked like the study of some Victorian English gentleman. The small, dapper Japanese who stood up behind the mammoth oak desk bowed not at all like an Englishman, then waved them to high-backed chairs that were more like thrones.

"The interior minister tells me you have some problem I may be able to help you with, Mr. Ambassador," the man said in perfect English, then seemed to see Carter and Siobhan for the first time. "Ah, so sorry. I am Ando Takeda, Managing Director of Takeda Research Limited. You are—?"

"Commanders Carter and O'Neill," the ambassador said. "Commander Carter is from our Department of Defense Intelligence service, and Commander O'Neill from Australian Naval Intelligence, managing director."

"Many military ancestors in my family," Takeda said, waving to a large portrait on the wall behind his desk. "The great Takeda Shingen, lord of the Takeda clan in the sixteenth century. He was the greatest soldier of his day. But that was long ago. What can Takeda help with now?"

"We understand Takeda Research is heavily involved in research and even production of food from the sea," Siobhan said.

"Ah! Food, chemicals, clothing, everything! The sea will be the new frontier for humanity. Perhaps we will even live under the sea. Live and farm and manufacture!"

Carter lifted the carrying case up onto the managing director's desk, opened the latched cover, and took out the sealed glass container. Ando Takeda stared at it. Siobhan opened the other carrying case and placed the second glass container beside the first. Both contained moving, writhing, snakelike stalks and leaves of seaweed, the containers almost choked with the mass of still growing plant that threatened to burst the ultra-strong tempered glass.

Carter told him what it was and where it had been found, leaving out the poison and fast growth. But Takeda could see the speed of growth for himself.

"It is growing in those containers!" he breathed.

"It's growing," Carter confirmed. "Do you recognize the plant? Anything about it, sir?"

Takeda leaned closer, stared, and began to nod. "Ah, yes, it looks very much like an excellent experimental specimen we have been working on for many years. Very high protein source, very strong in minerals, and very fast in growth. We have great hopes for it, but . . . but this is not quite the same, no. The color is darker, the leaf nodules are different. Similar, perhaps the same basic plant, but not exactly."

"Have you ever had any trouble with the plants you are working on?" Siobhan said.

"No."

"No accidents?" Carter asked.

"No."

"Some unusual incident in a small bay near Arao on Kyushu?" Siobhan said.

The managing director stared at them. "No. But we have our research facilities for underwater farming on the island of Ushi-shima in the Ariakeno-umi near Arao." He looked suddenly stern and angry. He turned to the ambassador. "You are not telling me something. What is it you know that you are not telling me, Mr. Ambassador?"

"I regret, Mr. Takeda, that we are not at liberty to divulge the nature of our inquiry even to you at this juncture. Be assured we have cleared this with your Interior Ministry, who feel that to involve anyone else prematurely would be a mistake and possibly dangerous to you and your company."

Takeda narrowed his eyes fiercely but said nothing. He didn't like being in the dark, but he was a Japanese and superior authority had spoken. He would obey until it became clear exactly where his own interests lay.

"Can you tell us if any incident has occurred and been hushed up at your research facilities on Ushi-shima?" Carter asked quietly.

"Hushed up? I would not hush up any incident of the type I assume you are suggesting! A dangerous incident."

"Could something have gone wrong without your being told?" Siobhan said.

Takeda seemed to turn to stone for an instant, his dark eyes as fierce as those of any sixteenth-century shogun. Then he pressed a button on his desk. The efficient secretary appeared. Takeda was so angry he lapsed into Japanese.

"Prepare my aircraft for immediate takeoff!"

She left as fast as she had come. Takeda turned his cold eyes on Carter, Siobhan, and the ambassador.

"We will go to Ushi-shima and find out."

"Er," the ambassador began, "immediately, sir?"

"Yes."

"I'm afraid I can't—"

"We'll take over, Mr. Ambassador," Carter said. He turned to Takeda. "Whenever you're ready, Mr. Takeda."

Ando Takeda bowed his head stiffly to Carter. "Now, Commander Carter."

They left the ambassador to find his own way out and down to his limousine. Takeda led them to a different private elevator: they rode up instead of down. At the top they were met by two men in plainclothes, clearly bodyguards and clearly armed. Takeda led the way in hard, determined strides for such a small man across the roof of the highrise to a waiting helicopter on its pad. A pilot held the door open for Takeda, Siobhan, and Carter, the rotors already turning. They ducked and climbed aboard. The two bodyguards climbed into the front with the pilots.

Takeda barked in Japanese, "Go!"

The helicopter lifted and swung steeply away across the teeming city. The snow-capped peak of Mount Fuji

towered in the noontime sky as the helicopter flew
straight toward Tokyo International. There they landed
in a restricted area and hurried across to a waiting
twin-engine executive jet marked with the Takeda
emblem. The two silent bodyguards, who were obviously Takeda's private protection, went on first, then
Takeda nodded Siobhan and Carter aboard.

The jet took off and headed southwest across the neat
fields of Honshu and almost directly over the great
white peak of Fuji-san to the Kwanto Plain that had
been the cradle of Japanese imperial power in the ancient capital of Nara and the city of Kyoto to the north
as they passed over Osaka and went out across the Inland Sea. Freighters and fishing boats dotted the great
expanse of almost landlocked water that had played
such an important role in Japanese history.

The smaller island of Shikoku passed quickly under
the jet, and then they crossed the other entrance to the
Inland Sea, the Hoyo-kaikyo, crossed Kyushu, and
reached the private Takeda Research airfield at the town
of Arao on the shore of the Ariakeno-umi. Another
helicopter was waiting for them and took them out
across the water to a small island with long low
buildings, many piers and boats, and great floating
racks and cribs of growing plants as far as Carter and
Siobhan could see.

A small group of white-coated men waited at the
helipad, one standing slightly in front of the others, all
looking excited, nervous, worried, and awed all at the
same time. The two bodyguards were first off the chopper. Ando Takeda went next like a lord of the clan
returning from the imperial court to his fief, his
stewards and retainers all waiting to greet him. For all
the modernity, and the disaster of the war, a lot had not
changed. In Japan, the ancient ways died slowly and
hard.

The man in front stepped farther forward, bowed his
head sharply to Takeda and began to speak in rapid
Japanese.

"Research Director Fukoa, Mr. Takeda. We are

honored the managing director comes to view our humble work. In what way can we help?"

"It is I who am honored, Research Director Fukoa. You can tell me if there has been some great problem here in the last year that I, perhaps, have not heard of?"

The research director seemed to hesitate, then bowed again. "No problem has been reported here that the managing director has not been informed of."

Takeda turned to Carter. "Commanders Carter, O'Neill."

It was Siobhan who stepped forward with her carrying case, opened it, and held up the glass container.

"*Ahhhhhhhhgggggggggggggg!!*"

The cry came from all the white-coated men ranged in a polite line behind the research director. Sharp, loud, involuntary, it echoed across the small island and buildings.

The research director seemed to almost stagger as he stared in horror.

FOURTEEN

Research Director Fukoa stared at the writhing plants inside the sealed containers. His shaking voice was hoarse.

"No. Not possible. No," he croaked in Japanese.

The line of white-coated scientists behind him could only mutter among themselves, their frightened eyes on the glass container and its seaweed. It was obvious they recognized the plant too.

"You all recognize the plant," Carter said.

"What is not possible, Fukoa?" Takeda demanded. "What is the lie you have been hiding?"

The trembling man didn't seem to hear either of them. He stared at the container and went on talking as if to some unseen ghost. "All destroyed, all gone. It is not possible. They say all destroyed, all gone. No way it could come back. No . . ."

"Who destroyed the plant?" Carter asked.

"Where did it come from?" Siobhan added.

"What did you hide, Fukoa?" Takeda barked. "What have you all hidden from the company? From me! A conspiracy!"

One of the men behind the staring, trembling director stepped forward, his face set more strongly than the others. A young man, not yet that afraid of the managing director.

"We could do nothing else, Managing Director. The prime minister himself swore us all to secrecy, a matter of national security."

"The prime minister?" Takeda said, astonished.

"How did the government become involved?" Carter said.

Takeda became even angrier. "You reported to the government, to the prime minister, before your company? Before *me?*"

"No," the young scientist said, holding his ground. "The government discovered the danger before we did."

Fukoa, the research director, came out of his trance and nodded to the young scientist. "Perhaps we should all go into the conference room, Managing Director, and I will tell you the whole story."

"Perhaps," Ando Takeda said, tight-lipped, "that would be a good thing to do."

Siobhan returned the glass container to its carrying case, and they all walked in silence into the main building of the research complex. Fukoa led them into a Western-style conference room where shoes could be worn but kimono-clad women immediately began to serve tea in small porcelain cups emblazoned with the ancient Takeda clan emblem. Fukoa stared at the floor as he began to talk.

"A year ago we were continuing our work on the original strain of this plant. It was our most promising source of food from the sea, its rate of growth being the best of those with high nutritional value. So when the American NASA asked us if we would like to participate in one of their space shuttle trips, you will recall, Managing Director, that we chose to send a sample of the plant to test the effect of space radiation on it."

"I do not recall," Takeda said, "but it does not matter. Get to the point, Dr. Fukoa."

The research director took a deep breath. "When the sample plants and seeds were returned from the space experiment, we continued to observe and grow them here." He looked up at Takeda, his eyes haunted. "Almost at once we noticed a difference. The plants, and those that grew from the seeds we had sent into space, developed differences in configuration and appearance, and began to grow at an incredible rate. We had never seen anything like it. They grew so fast you could see them growing!

"We were elated, and transferred the mutant plants to large tanks sunk into the seawater of the Ariakenoumi. They continued to grow fantastically, wonderfully!" Fukoa looked up and around at all of them: his colleagues, Ando Takeda, Carter, and Siobhan O'Neill. "Then it happened. We had always, of course, handled the specimens with sterile gloves, under sterile conditions, in hoods and glove boxes. This is normal practice on experimental samples. So when we transferred the plants to the open tanks in the sea, they were exposed to the external world for the first time."

The haunted look in Fukoa's eyes changed to one of remembered terror. "Fish began to die. We found them floating near the tanks immediately. One of the men who transferred the plants to the tanks became ill and died within hours. The plants grew so fast they began to spread out of the tanks. It all happened so fast—overnight—that it was the defense force patrol boat that saw the dead fish first and alerted us. When they heard about the new plants, they immediately notified Tokyo. The prime minister himself ordered all the plants destroyed immediately, and ordered all of us to remain silent."

"Without notifying your superiors?" Takeda said. "He did not have that right!"

"He said he did, Managing Director. He spoke of the great fear among the people if it were ever known, of the importance of the sea to Japan. So we remained silent."

"Can we see the records of the experiments?" Carter asked.

Fukoa shook his head. "All records were destroyed. All data about the mutant plants—everything that related to the plants or had touched the plants—was destroyed and we were all sworn to silence."

The word echoed in a silence of its own. No one spoke in the elegant room, the only sound the soft padding of the slippered feet of the waitresses serving tea and small cakes. It was Carter who finally broke the silence.

"Then where did these plants come from?" he said. "Was anyone else working on the same plants?"

"No, it was a development hybrid of Takeda alone. No one else sent it into space. The American NASA is very careful not to duplicate experiments."

"Someone must have been duplicating your work," Siobhan said. "Perhaps another research installation in Takeda Research itself, Mr. Takeda?"

Ando Takeda shook his head. "That would not be economical, Commander. All our sea and underwater research is done here."

"Is there anyone who could have kept a set of records —someone who might not have destroyed them?" Carter asked.

"No," Fukoa said.

"Was there one of you who worked more closely on this project than anyone else?" Carter pursued.

This time the silence was heavy among the Japanese research scientists. Fukoa nodded.

"Yes. Dr. Tetsu Ashekagi, our most honored botanist, supervised the entire project. But he could not have kept back any records or informed anyone of the project."

"Why?" Carter said.

"Because, Commander Carter, he died in a tragic accident a week after all trace of the deadly mutation was destroyed."

"Accident?" Carter said.

"What kind of accident, Dr. Fukoa?" Siobhan asked.

Both their voices were heavy with suspicion. Coincidence was not something that happened often in their trade.

"Ah, I understand what you think," Fukoa said, "but there can be no doubt. Dr. Ashekagi was out in the specimen launch looking for a reported colony of shellfish not usually found this far north when the boat struck some underwater object and sank. The doctor must have hit his head. His body was found a week later some thirty miles north of here with a heavy wound on the head. Most tragic. He was a man of great knowledge."

"You're sure it was his body?" Siobhan said.

"Absolutely. We all identified it. His family also identified him. The head wound was the only disfigurement."

Carter rubbed his chin. "A week after the accident? Was the body where you would have expected it to be in that time?"

Fukoa nodded. "The defense forces were most careful in their investigation; they too were suspicious."

"Could he have taken any records of his work with him?"

"No. All were absolutely destroyed."

"And every specimen? Every seed?"

"Absolutely."

Carter nodded slowly, then glanced at Siobhan. She was looking at him. But it was Ando Takeda who spoke.

"Then how do these specimens in the jars exist, Dr. Fukoa?"

Fukoa shook his head, almost in despair. "I do not know, Managing Director."

"Perhaps some samples were stolen before you discovered their danger? Perhaps in the United States? On the space shuttle?" Takeda suggested.

Fukoa sighed miserably. "No, Managing Director. The samples were all carefully coded and controlled. There is no doubt we received back all we had given to the shuttle experiment."

"Dammit!" Takeda suddenly exploded. "These samples in the containers came from somewhere! Are you suggesting that someone else performed an exact duplicate experiment?"

"I don't know what to suggest," Fukoa said, looking at them all now. "I have no answer. There is no answer I can see!"

"There's always an answer," Carter said. "No matter how unexpected or impossible. All we have to do is find it. May we inspect the laboratory where the initial work was done? And Dr. Ashekagi's laboratory?"

"Of course," Fukoa said. "But there is only one to inspect. All the work was done in Dr. Ashekagi's own laboratory."

Carter turned to Ando Takeda. "We'd like to do it alone if you don't object, Mr. Takeda."

The leader of the Takeda clan and the company fixed his employee scientists with a cold eye. Some of them swallowed hard.

"Of course," Takeda said. "I wish to talk to my people anyway, and to the prime minister."

Fukoa led Carter and Siobhan O'Neill out of the main building and through the shaded grounds to a distant smaller building. Inside, the building was one large room with a glassed-in smaller laboratory in the far corner. It was empty and silent.

"The prime minister ordered it closed for the year," Fukoa said. "Now no one wishes to work in here. Perhaps the managing director will correct such superstition."

"Meanwhile," Carter said, "it is exactly as it was left by Dr. Ashekagi?"

"No. As it was left by the defense troops after they searched and destroyed everything."

Carter and Siobhan thanked the research director,

who left somewhat unhappily. He was not looking forward to his "family" discussion with Ando Takeda. And they were not looking forward to searching the laboratory of the late Dr. Ashekagi.

"Not much chance," Siobhan said.

"No, they'll have swept it clean and polished the air," Carter agreed. "Still, let's take a look."

They looked.

And came up with nothing.

"They didn't even leave any dust," Carter said.

"No," Siobhan agreed, but she was staring at a large nautical chart in Dr. Ashekagi's private laboratory. It was hung over his desk and was surrounded by snapshots of two smiling men sailing a medium-sized sailboat. The chart was the kind used by yachtsmen when sailing inland waterways.

"It's the Ariakeno-umi," Siobhan said. "A complete chart of the waters. I'm a bit of a sailing enthusiast. This is the kind of chart a regular pleasure sailor uses, and it shows every reef and rock in the entire area."

"Meaning Ashekagi was an experienced sailor in these waters and should have known every pebble, rock, and ripple like a book."

"That's what I'd say. Look at all the photos of him sailing the bay."

"So what did he hit and why?"

"It's a good question."

"We'd better talk to his family."

Siobhan nodded. They left the laboratory and crossed through the wooded grounds of the remote and isolated research island back to the conference hall. They could hear the loud, harsh tones of Ando Takeda tongue-lashing his "family" for their misplaced loyalties in obeying the government's orders over their duty to inform their own leader of what had happened. This was not for outsiders, and as soon as Carter and Siobhan appeared, Takeda abruptly dismissed the scientists, informed them he would be staying a few days, perhaps longer, and would inspect all their work.

"Ah, you have had success?" the managing director said as he turned smoothly to Carter and Siobhan with a pleasant, natural smile.

"Not much," Siobhan said.

"Only that Dr. Ashekagi seems to have known the waters around here like a book. He had a detailed chart of every possible rock and reef on his wall, and probably in his head," Carter said. "It seems strange he would collide with something, and so violently and unexpectedly that he fell and hit his head hard enough to knock him out while the boat sank."

"So?" Takeda said.

"Where can we talk to Dr. Ashekagi's family?"

Takeda turned sharply. "Fukoa!"

The research director had almost made it out of the conference room. He seemed to wilt under the bark, and turned wearily back. "Yes, Managing Director?"

"Where is Dr. Ashekagi's family?"

"They live in Arao, Managing Director."

"You will take Commander Carter and Commander O'Neill to see them."

"Of course, Managing Director. I will call immediately and make the arrangements. Madame Ashekagi is still in seclusion, but I am sure she will see us when I explain that you request the visit."

Fukoa left to make the call. Takeda bowed to Carter and Siobhan. "Rooms will be ready in the guesthouse when you return. You are our guests as long as you wish to remain. Perhaps you will do me the honor of joining me for tea later?"

"We will be honored, Mr. Takeda," Siobhan said.

Fukoa returned and reported that Madame Ashekagi would see Carter and Siobhan as Mr. Takeda wished. Takeda left, and Fukoa seemed to brighten at once, to turn into a different man—brisk, in charge.

"A boat is at the dock now if you are ready."

They followed Fukoa back to the dock and rode across the Ariakeno-umi. At the village dock Dr. Fukoa took them to a small Honda sedan. The home of the

Ashekagi family was a large Japanese-style house with an outer courtyard entered through a solid gate in a street wall. Fukoa rang and a servant in a kimono opened the outer door and ushered them into the courtyard.

As the gate closed behind them, seven men in black kimonos, wearing white headbands emblazoned with red characters, a pair of samurai swords thrust into their sashes, appeared all around Carter, Siobhan, and Fukoa.

"What . . . what . . . do you . . . ?" Fukoa stammered, stepping toward the tallest of the men in the black kimonos.

The long sword seemed to shine in the afternoon sun without even being drawn, without the swordsman seeming to move. The long sword, a *katana*, in his hand as if by magic, sliced through the air, its end pointed high into the sky, silver and dripping red as Fukoa's head fell to the dirt of the courtyard while his body stood for a second longer before falling beside it.

FIFTEEN

Wilhelmina cut down the sword-wielding warrior in the black kimono and red-lettered headband who leaped at Carter.

Siobhan had her small Walther PPK. She shot the swordsman attacking her. But the black-garbed man grunted, scowled, and kept coming on toward her.

A second man was on Carter with incredible speed, the shining arc of the *katana* aimed at Carter's neck. Carter went in under the hiss of the sword. The swordsman kicked Wilhelmina from his hand. From his crouch, Carter chopped the swordsman's supporting leg, sending him crashing to the courtyard dirt. Rolling, the man drew his *wakizashi* short sword and came up in a single motion. Carter snatched the long *katana* from the hand of the man he'd shot dead.

Siobhan shot again. The attacker grunted again, his sword sweeping so close under her chin she fell backward to the dirt, her Walther knocked from her hand. With a savage cry the wounded man closed in, hurled himself at her with his failing strength, and flew over her head as she caught his chest with both feet and flung him over her, his sword driving into the dirt of the courtyard, his body hanging from the hilt more dead than alive.

Charging, the attacker with the *wakizashi* parried Carter's lethal slash of his borrowed sword, ducked under, and came up in a liquid flow with the short sword plunging toward Carter's heart. Carter spun, dropping him with a high kick to the chin, the neck snapping so loudly, it echoed through the courtyard.

The four remaining attackers pressed in.

Siobhan grabbed a long *katana*.

They faced, four against two.

The tall leader who had killed Dr. Fukoa spoke sharply to his men in Japanese, assuming that the Caucasians would not understand him.

"Full battle tactics! These two are trained with guns and swords. Kill or die for the honor of Fujiwara. Go!"

The four spread out, two facing Carter and two now advancing on Siobhan. The tall leader himself moved slowly toward Carter as if he had decided on the most dangerous adversary, the place of greatest honor. Carter smiled, and focused not on the man's hands but his feet.

"It is an honor to face the Fujiwara," Carter said in Japanese.

The tall leader answered in English. "So? You speak Japanese and know of the great Fujiwara clan. Perhaps it will not be without honor to kill you."

"A samurai who fights for a clan of courtiers has little honor to defend," Carter said, watching the second man inch to his left, the other two moving slowly to take Siobhan from two sides.

The tall leader's face darkened. "The Fujiwara are now samurai! The greatest family of the ancients is now the greatest family of the future! The clan that will renew the blood of Japan, of the world!"

The second man was almost level with Carter now, between Carter and Siobhan. The two stalking Siobhan moved in ever closer to where she waited with the samurai sword resting on her shoulder like nothing more deadly than a garden tool. Only the tall leader had not moved, momentarily distracted by Carter's taunting.

"By killing unarmed scientists?" Carter laughed. "The act of a peasant!"

The tall leader smiled. "A feeble attempt to provoke me, American. You have studied—"

The second man's jaw muscles tensed to make his move. Carter swung his sword up and feinted a lunge at the tall leader. The second man saw his chance and leaped in. Carter whirled in the motion of feinting back in the opposite direction to slice open the belly of the second man whose sword came down on empty air, his guts and blood pouring out across the ground. The second man already on his knees and dying, the tall leader frozen in mid-smile with his sword up to repel the feinted attack that never came, Carter stood five yards away, legs apart, sword out, watching the one man dying and the other a momentarily frozen statue.

The two attacking Siobhan made their moves at the same instant on some unseen signal. Unseen by anyone except Siobhan herself. In the split second between their standing poised and the swift motion of attack, her long samurai *katana* came off her shoulder and she darted sideways toward the attacker on the left. The swift, unexpected move, timed to take advantage of her opponent's force moving in the opposite direction, brought her behind the arc of his sword before he knew she had even moved, and out of the reach of the sword of the other attacker on her right.

The Australian plunged the *katana* into the attacker in front of her, withdrew as he dropped in a fountain of his own blood, and turned on the survivor feet apart, sword forward, in a duplication of Carter's stance.

The four faced each other, the two surviving black-robed attackers now aware they were not up against amateur swordsmen.

No one moved.

Shifted feet.

Watched.

Shuffled closer.

Held.

And the black-garbed attacker facing Siobhan broke first, rushing forward with a violent cry. His sword flashed down but sliced only empty air as the blood poured from the cut across his neck made by her faster sword that caught the final slash of his blade and twisted the sword from his already dead hands.

The tall leader strode forward. Carter met him. Their blades clashed, rang, flashed in the late evening sun, circled, and thrust. The tall leader of the attackers was a master swordsman. He parried all Carter's attacks but could make no headway against the skill of the Killmaster.

Siobhan came up behind the tall man in the black kimono. The man pivoted and backed toward the courtyard wall to keep them both in front of him.

"You've fought enough," Carter said.

The leader smiled. "I have two swords, American."

He continued to back toward the wall, and stumbled over the barely alive body of the first man Siobhan had cut down. Carter took the small opening, thrust and cut, and drew blood from the tall man's right arm and knocked away his *katana*.

With only his *wakizashi* in his left hand, the man nodded. "So?"

"You can't win now. Tell us who sent you," Carter said.

"No," the man said in English, pressing his bloody right arm against the black kimono. "I cannot win now. A pity. You are master swordsmen. I underestimated you both."

"It happens."

"I have failed my lord. You will both die soon. I shall merely be first."

Before they could move, the tall man slashed down with the *wakizashi* in both hands and decapitated his still twitching comrade, then cut his own throat in a

single slash and fell to the courtyard, his blood
spreading in a pool around him.

Carter and Siobhan watched him die, his *wakizashi*
pointed toward them in case they tried to save him, a
smile slowly fading into the rictus of death.

They looked slowly around at the eight bodies that littered the courtyard. They moved from one to the other,
looking for a sign of life. All were dead. Siobhan tossed
her long *katana* away.

"He didn't want to risk being questioned," she said.

"No," Carter agreed. "Those red symbols on the
headbands are the Fujiwara crest."

"But the Fujiwara rule ended in the twelfth century,
Nick. As far as I know, there isn't any Fujiwara clan
anymore."

"No, but someone is using the crest, and not for
fun." He glanced around the bloody courtyard with its
severed heads and dead bodies. "Where the hell's the
family we came to talk to?"

He strode across the courtyard to the front door of
the Japanese-style house and knocked loudly. He
knocked again on the doorframe with the hilt of the
borrowed *katana* sword.

"You go away," a shaking voice said at last from
behind the closed door. "You go."

"Open the door or I'll cut it down!" Carter said. He
motioned to Siobhan to pick up one of the swords that
littered the yard. She nodded, and retrieved the blood-
iest.

There was a whispered conversation in frantic
Japanese behind the closed door. Then it slowly slid
open. Carter and Siobhan kicked off their shoes and
entered warily, their bloody *katanas* out in front of
them.

The interior was dim, shades drawn. Seven or eight
indistinct figures stood in a line on the far side of the
room as if they wanted to stay as far from the con-
tamination of Carter and Siobhan as possible. Their
eyes caught the stray beams of muted light through the

drawn shades, shined like the eyes of small animals hiding in corners.

As Carter's eyes grew accustomed to the dim interior, he saw a woman in her thirties in the center, with two slightly younger men on either side, all dressed in Western clothes. An elderly couple in traditional Japanese attire stood on the left, each holding the hand of a small child in Japanese dress. The final figure was a boy in his early teens wearing a school uniform. They were all utterly terrified, shaking where they stood. Only the teen-age boy didn't shake, his eyes bolder than the rest, a little defiant, staring at the bloody swords.

"Mrs. Ashekagi?" Carter said.

It was as if they didn't hear him. Only the boy, whose eyes flickered up, watched Carter almost curiously. The others stood frozen yet trembling, their eyes searching in every direction. They did not look at the bloody swords as the boy did; they looked everywhere else as if expecting some terror to appear and strike them down. Not Carter and Siobhan, some other terror. Someone or something else.

"Why were we attacked by those Fujiwara men? Who were they?" Carter asked.

The name said aloud seemed to make them shake even more. They stared at Carter and Siobhan with a kind of horror.

"You kill," one of the men flanking the woman said in English. "Why you kill? Now we all die!"

"We killed them because they wanted to kill us," Carter said in Japanese. "Why will you die because we killed them? Why did they attack us?"

They were all dumbfounded to hear Carter speak Japanese, and stared at him. The boy blinked, fascinated.

"They didn't want us to talk to you," the boy said. "You killed them all! How can an American be a samurai? How can a woman?"

"They were protecting you, then," Carter said. "Why? What are they to you? Who are they?"

"They bring us—" the boy began.

"Quiet! Say nothing!" the old man barked sharply.

The second younger man said, his frightened voice hoarse, "You go away. We not talk to you."

Siobhan suddenly looked around the large room. "This is an expensive house with beautiful things. You're living well, all of you. How?"

The widow of Dr. Ashekagi spoke for the first time. "We have a pension. The company is most generous."

"No," Carter said. "Japanese companies take care of their employees, but not that well. Why were those men protecting you from us? What do you know they didn't want you to tell us?"

"What is someone paying you off for?" Siobhan demanded. "The secret of the mutant seaweed plant?"

"Or," Carter said, "to keep silent about the week between your husband's accident and his death? Blood money?"

Mrs. Ashekagi fainted. The two younger men stared at Carter, terrified out of their minds. The teen-age boy ran to his fallen mother and looked up at Carter with tears in his eyes. The old man stepped closer to Carter and Siobhan.

"My son is dead. Have you no respect for the dead? Leave us in peace."

"We respect the dead," Carter said, "but we have to help the living. That mutant plant is loose in the world, do you understand? Your son's work has been stolen by someone who plans to use it as a weapon. Who has it? Who killed your son?"

"Go away," the old man said. "We know nothing."

"They will kill us," one of the younger men said.

"My sister is alone now," the other younger man said. "They help her. She will not talk to you."

Their terror was too deep. Terror and need. They wouldn't talk no matter how long Carter and Siobhan waited. Carter nodded to the Australian agent. They dropped their long samurai *katana* swords, went out into the courtyard where the bodies lay silent, picked up their guns, and walked through the outer gate to Fukoa's Honda.

"Someone is paying them off," Siobhan said.

"Whoever's using the Fujiwara crest," Carter said. "We'd better report to Takeda and let him tell the police about Fukoa and those men. Maybe he'll have some ideas on who these Fujiwara samurai were."

They drove back to the pier where the Takeda Research boat waited. The crew looked for Dr. Fukoa. Carter shook his head.

"He won't be coming back." He told them of Dr. Fukoa's murder. "Take us—"

The Killmaster stopped. He was facing the cabin window of the motor cruiser. Reflected in the glass he saw a car parked off the road behind some trees where anyone seated in it could observe the boat. The car had a long antenna, and even as he looked he saw someone inside raise something to his face and move his head as if talking.

They were being watched and reported on!

SIXTEEN

The man in the car hidden behind the grove of trees lowered the radiophone. Carter continued to watch the reflection in the window. The car was too far away to make out more than the shapes.

"Nick?" Siobhan said.

Carter laughed, turned from the window, and pointed out across the open water as if he'd spotted something amusing.

"There's a car watching us from behind a grove of trees up the road. At least two men. Using a radiophone to report to someone."

Siobhan laughed and seemed to appreciate the distant event. "Police?"

"I don't think so. They're not good enough at covering themselves, and the car's a Mercedes."

"Who then? Our Fujiwara?"

"That's what I'd guess."

"They got here fast."

"Watching all along, or the Ashekagis reported us."

"Grab the birds?"

"Follow them back to the nest."

Siobhan laughed again and took Carter's hand. "How?"

"I've got a homer in my equipment. We'll need a decoy."

"You or me?"

"Take your pick."

"I'll decoy. I always wanted to be an actress."

They strolled to the front of the boat, out of sight of the hidden car. Carter removed the tiny electronic transmitter from the equipment pouch inside his camouflage fatigues and strapped the small receiver that looked like a watch onto his wrist. He checked to make sure they were operating.

"How do you want to handle it?" Carter asked.

"If we separate, they might try to follow both of us."

"But that would alert them, make them suspicious," Carter said. "Let's go back ashore together and separate where they can't see us. Come on."

They told the boatmen to wait until they returned, walked back onshore, and turned left on the road toward the center of the town. They strolled easily, like two tourists sampling the exotic scene of rural Japan off the beaten track. The Mercedes soon appeared behind them, driving casually along the road. Once in the busy early evening streets of the town itself, Carter looked for what he wanted: somewhere he would be out of sight of the Mercedes but where Siobhan would be in plain sight talking to him.

He found it in a small photographer's shop where the rural cameraman specialized in taking postcard portraits of tourists against fake Japanese backdrops. The shop was so small Siobhan had to stand outside while Carter was inside being photographed against a Japanese garden painted on cardboard, and there was a back door.

Carter quickly explained what he wanted to the shop owner, gave him five thousand yen, put on a prop kimono where he could be seen, went inside, and slipped out the rear door while the photographer pretended to be taking his picture and Siobhan stood outside the shop talking to him. She carried on an animated conversation with the nonexistent Carter inside the shop.

The Killmaster circled through the backyards and alleys of the town until he calculated he was behind the Mercedes, then moved silently back to the main street. The black car was half a block away, parked where anyone in it could see Siobhan talking to him inside the shop. But they wouldn't be able to see inside without getting too close and risk being spotted.

Carter noticed that there were only two men in the car, both in the front seat. One spoke from time to time into the hand-held radio. Both smoked. They were watchful, alert to Siobhan and the unseen Carter, but not alert enough. They were so sure their target was in front of them they didn't even glance at the other cars and bicycles and people that passed.

The Killmaster motioned to a man wearing an old-fashioned wide straw hat shaped like a flat cone and bought the hat from him. He let the man walk on, then he stepped out of the alley and strode toward the rear of the car. The hat hiding his face, his knees bent to disguise his height, Carter blended easily with the hurrying throngs of Japanese. As he passed the car he bent his knees lower, slipped the magnetic homer under the rear bumper, and walked on.

The two men in the car paid no attention to him, smoking and relaxing in the false security of knowing exactly where their quarry was. Amateurs, Carter decided as he walked past the photographer's shop and turned the next corner into a cross street of the town. From there he worked his way quickly back to the rear of the photographer's shop, took off the kimono, and appeared at the door paying the photographer and showing the supposed postcard photos to Siobhan.

"Done?" she said.

"Done. Now back to the boat and send it off."

"I presume that means a swim?"

"I've missed the water."

"We should have been fish."

They strolled back along the main street after giving

the Mercedes time to back away, turn a corner, and wait until they had passed to start along behind them again.

"They're not so good," Siobhan said.

"No," Carter agreed. "An amateur operation."

"Those soldiers on Kwaj weren't amateurs," she said. "And the swordsmen."

"Or the raiders on New Guinea. We've got a mixed bag."

"Trained soldiers but not trained intelligence agents or policemen."

They reached the dock and boarded the boat once more, aware of the Mercedes back in its grove of trees in the fading evening light. On board, they walked forward out of sight of the trees. The head crewman of Takeda Research looked at the low sun, the already darkening day.

"It is getting late, Commander Carter. We should return to the island soon."

"Yes," Carter said. "I want you to take the boat back now. Commander O'Neill and I will stay behind. Tell Managing Director Takeda that we have work to do and we'll get back on our own, or we'll contact the island when we want to be picked up."

"You will stay behind?"

"With Dr. Fukoa's car. Please tell Mr. Takeda."

"He will be told at once," the crewman said. "You are going ashore now?"

"Not until you're on your way."

Carter explained what he wanted done. The crewman went off to start the boat's engines. Carter and Siobhan returned to the stern where they sat on the low cabin and talked in plain sight of the watching Mercedes. The boat cast off and moved slowly out into the Ariakeno-umi in the twilight toward the Takeda Research island. Carter and Siobhan watched the grove of trees.

The Mercedes didn't move.

The boat sailed farther out into the open water.

One of the men in the Mercedes got out and stared toward the boat as it sailed on.

Carter and Siobhan walked forward out of sight of the shore. They quickly put their weapons, watches, and electronic equipment into the waterproof containers they hung around their necks, and slipped over the bow of the moving boat. They sank deep at once to escape the propellors as the boat passed over them, then swam as far as they could underwater and surfaced slowly without a ripple.

The one man was still standing beside the almost hidden Mercedes and watching the boat as it sailed on toward the island.

Carter and Siobhan sank again and swam on underwater toward shore. They surfaced in shallow water under the dock and raised their heads cautiously. The Mercedes was driving away.

The instant it was out of sight they climbed up and ran to Dr. Fukoa's Honda. Dripping seawater, Siobhan drove. Carter opened his waterproof container and strapped the electronic receiver to his wrist. The signals came in strong and directly ahead. They followed through the dusk.

It was completely dark before the Mercedes turned off the main highway.

"They're turning back toward the Ariakeno-umi," Carter said. He watched the directional signals on his electronic scanner, and saw the dark side road as they reached it. "This is it."

Siobhan turned right in the night. The signal was again straight ahead. They drove on until the rising moon reflected from water through the trees, and the Mercedes came to a halt somewhere ahead in the night. Siobhan stopped and turned off the headlights. Carter watched the scanner on his wrist. Siobhan listened.

"About half a mile," Carter said. "Holding steady."

"Too far to hear, but I can see light off to the right that could be headlights."

"I think they're home."

"The lights just went off."

"Let's move."

Out of the car they advanced through the trees. If there were any sentries, they would watch the road. The scanner led them straight ahead to the edge of the water. The Mercedes was parked just off the road. It was dark and empty. There was no one around it in the moonlight. A dock protruded out into the Ariakeno-umi. It was closed off by a locked gate. The running lights of a boat bobbed on the water, a silvery wake leading back to the dock.

"They're on that boat," Siobhan said.

"And there's an island not far off out there," Carter said. "Dr. Ashekagi ran into his accident off an island."

"Another swim?"

"Good exercise," Carter said and grinned. "Only let's keep our clothes dry this time. It gets cold later."

They stripped naked and rolled their fatigues up small enough to fit into the waterproof containers with their pistols and electronic equipment. They looked at each other for a moment, smiled, and entered the water. They swam easily in the moonlight, the water silver and the running lights of the boat ahead slowly fading and finally vanishing as they saw the dark shape of a rocky island loom black in the night. As they swam closer, the outlines of a low headland separated itself from the larger mass of the island and revealed a narrow cove behind it.

The boat was tied up to a dock inside the cove, all its lights and the dock itself dark. They swam slowly into the cove as the water grew shallower. A faint path led upward in the moonlight from the dock and vanished among thick trees. Faint light showed through the trees.

Siobhan stroked slowly in the dark water of the cove. "There's a house up there."

They swam in without a ripple. There was no one on the dock or path. They dried off as best they could and put on their clothes. At the top they surveyed the small, rustic Japanese house with the light soft through the rice-paper screens of the windows. Someone was kneeling in the main room, or *shiroshoin*, at the *shoin* writing alcove on the raised *jodan no ma* section. Carter and Siobhan circled the little four-room house and saw no sign of anyone else. The whole island was no more than a single large hill, and there were no other lights anywhere.

"Where'd they go?" Siobhan wondered.

"Two from the Mercedes, and there had to be crew on the boat," Carter said. "Let's find out."

They walked boldly up to the small house and knocked on the outer door. They heard soft footsteps, and the door was opened by a compact man wearing old-fashioned Japanese-style clothes. He smiled in delight as he saw them.

"Ah, please come in," he said in English. "Travelers are always welcome in my house."

Carter and Siobhan removed their shoes and went into the living room built in the old style as a *shiroshoin*. Their smiling host motioned them to sit on cushions set on the mats at low tables lacquered in delicate reds and black.

"You will take tea?"

He did not wait for an answer but went out into the kitchen section where a kettle was already boiling, and he made a pot of tea in the English fashion without ceremony. He brought their cups—English style with handles—milk, and sugar.

"Our tea ceremony is a profound ritual, but I have never seen any need to subject thirsty visitors to its rigors."

He took his own cup and went to sit on cushions on the raised platform. Carter studied him. His clothes weren't just any modern kimono.

He wore the *hitatare* of a high member of the warrior class of the Edo period of the Tokugawa shogunate; a sumptuous dark red upper garment like a short kimono with voluminous sleeves, and matching *hakama* trousers that trailed on the floor behind him. Under the heavy silk *hitatare* he wore a fine dark blue and white *noshime*

with gold decorations on the white midsection. His feet
were not visible as he walked or sat. His hair was shaved
except for a topknot tied and held by a gold clasp.

"So," he said, "to what do I owe the honor of this
visit to my humble island?"

Carter drank his tea. It was good and hot after their
swim.

"We followed two men in a Mercedes," he said in
English, "Mr.—?"

"Masashige," the man said, and bowed his head.
"You are?"

"Commander Carter, United States Navy, and Commander O'Neill of the Australian Navy."

"Ah? These men you follow—this is a military matter? Alas, I know little of military matters. I'm only a
humble scholar." And he waved to great rows of books
and manuscripts on the shelves of his *shoin* and across
the whole rear wall of the *tokonoma* alcove.

"The Mercedes was parked on the mainland,"
Siobhan said, "at a dock where a boat took the two men
to this island."

The man's eyes flickered for a second as he turned to
look at Siobhan when she spoke. "Here? That is not
possible. No one has come to this island. My boat has
not left for days."

"You're sure?" Carter said.

"I expect you have examined the island, Commander." Mr. Masashige smiled. "Have you found
those you followed, or any boat crew?"

"No," the Killmaster admitted.

"Ah." The man smiled again. "Probably the boat
you seek sailed around me and on to one of the larger
islands. I regret I can't help more."

Carter nodded, finished his tea, and stood up.
Siobhan looked at him but did the same, saying
nothing.

"We thank you, Mr. Masashige, for the tea and the
help."

"It is I who thank you for your visit. Perhaps you

would like to use my boat for your return trip. You may leave it at the mainland dock."

"That's very kind of you," Siobhan said.

They left the small, compact man standing in his doorway, looking in the *hitatare, noshime,* and shaved head like some ancient *daimyo*. The only thing missing were the pair of swords.

They walked back down the path in the moonlight to the silent boat at its dock in the hidden cove.

"Is he lying, Nick?" Siobhan said.

"Of course he's lying," Carter said. "He wasn't at all surprised to see us on his island, and he never asked us how we got to the island. Then he slipped and revealed he knew we didn't have a boat."

"He knew we swam out."

"Which means someone was watching the cove, and as soon as he saw us he guessed who we were. Which means he knew those two were watching us and realized at once we'd turned the tables."

They reached the boat. Carter opened the engine hatch and felt the engine.

"Still warm."

"What do we do?" Siobhan asked.

"Exactly what we said. Return to the mainland, leave the boat, and drive off."

"Then?"

"Then we come back underwater and find out what Mr. Masashige is really up to."

SEVENTEEN

They left the boat at the dock and drove back to
Arao. The Takeda Research boat was there waiting for
them.

"Mr. Takeda say come back, wait," the crew chief
explained.

The boat returned them to the Takeda island, and the
police were there to greet them. They listened politely in
the private office of the managing director as Carter and
Siobhan told their story of the murder of Dr. Fukoa and
the attack of the Fujiwara "samurai."

"The Ashekagi family must have given you the story
already," Siobhan said.

"Ashekagi family has disappeared," the police detective in charge said. "Also bodies of attackers. Only Dr.
Fukoa's body was in courtyard, and much blood."

"So you have no proof of our story," Carter said.

"There is the evidence of blood, and there were
witnesses," the detective said. "We do not doubt you,
Commander Carter."

Carter nodded. "Then they took the bodies and the
Ashekagis for some other reason than to try to deny
what happened."

"It would seem so," the detective agreed. "What

149

would you think that reason could be?''

"I have no idea," Carter said blandly.

"Nor I," Siobhan said.

"I see," the detective said. "Well, perhaps if you think of some reason, you will contact us."

They assured him they would, and the police left. Ando Takeda sat down and looked at them.

"So? You have no idea why the Ashekagis have vanished?"

"Let's just say our ideas are not for police consumption, Mr. Takeda," Carter said. "But we would like to talk to you if we could."

Takeda nodded. "Of course. But you must be hungry. And cold. Perhaps tea and sandwiches?"

Takeda pressed a button, and two of the kimono-clad waitresses appeared, listened to his order, and left. Takeda offered Carter and Siobhan a drink of sake. They declined and sat down. Carter leaned forward in his chair and told Takeda about the attack, the surveillance, and the small man in the rustic house on the island.

"He was dressed very elegantly, and in a very old-fashioned way," Carter finished. "Samurai clothes from at least two hundred years ago."

"Yes, he would be," Takeda said after a silence. "His name isn't Masashige, or only his given name is. The man you met on that island is Fujiwara Masashige himself."

"Fujiwara?" Siobhan said. "Those attackers—?"

Takeda nodded. "His private organization. Almost a private army, we in Japan sometimes think. But he is such a great man, so brilliant and honored, no one will speak out against him in public, and he has never been accused of anything violent. Until now, that is. I think the police will now ask some questions about what happened to you."

"Honored for what?" Carter asked.

"He is a brilliant journalist and international scholar of history, especially the *Sengoku jidai*, or the Japanese era of the country at war during the sixteenth century, and a radical philosopher who has taught and written all over the world. He is also an expert on Western literature and philosophy, and a master of kendo."

"A master swordsman, in other words," Carter said.

"Yes, he and all his followers practice kendo."

"What kind of radical philosophy does he espouse?" Siobhan asked.

Takeda thought. "That is difficult to explain. Perhaps his personal story will answer you. He is a direct descendant of the Fujiwara family, who, as you know, ruled Japan in the Heian period, the ninth to the twelfth centuries, or considerably longer than the Tokugawa shoguns. They were not a military family, but aristocrats at the court of the emperor in Kyoto, and while they had the same kind of power behind the throne as the Tokugawas, they did not take the title 'shogun.' "

The tea and sandwiches came, and Takeda waited until they were all served before going on. "His given name, Masashige, is that of one of our most famous, noble, and honorable samurai of the past, Kusunoke Masashige, and perhaps that is the best clue to his ideas. He was not given the name as a child but took it as an adult, and he always uses the true ancient order of Japanese names: Fujiwara Masashige. I, for example, in the past would have been called Takeda Ando, not the Westernized Ando Takeda."

"So," Carter said, "he is a man who believes in the past of Japan, the samurai ways, even the ancient imperial court ideals."

"More than that," Takeda said. "Simply put, Fujiwara Masashige has come to blame the evils of today on what he views as modern ways false to true human nature. He sees today as a corrupt time and wants to return to the old ways."

"By force?" Carter wondered.

"I did not think so," Takeda said, "but perhaps he has changed."

"Yes," Carter said.

"What will you do?"

"Find out," the Killmaster said. "And if he is behind the violence, stop him."

"That may not be so easy, Commander Carter."

"It never is," Carter said.

When they finished their sandwiches they excused themselves and went to the rooms prepared for them in the research complex. They looked at the beds and each other.

"Tonight?" Siobhan said.

"People are dying."

"Tonight," she said with a sigh. "Underwater again?"

"Someone spotted us swimming earlier, and a boat's easy to see at night."

"We didn't bring our own equipment."

"They must have scuba gear here. After all, it's a marine research installation."

"What if we run into that weed?"

"If Fujiwara is behind it, he wouldn't have it growing near his own base."

"When?"

"Now."

They found the scuba equipment in a diving room near the docks on the Ariakeno-umi, and told Takeda they wanted to use the boat again. Dressed in the borrowed wet suits, fins, masks, and air tanks, they boarded and directed the crew chief to sail as silently as possible toward the small island some miles up the coast.

The moon was down now, and the inland water was black, only the small light on the dials in the cabin breaking the night. The crew chief sailed slowly and carefully, watching the channel markers. He knew the waters like the back of his hand, but he still sailed cautiously, the motor barely turning over, almost inaudible in the blackness. But Carter took no chances. When they were in the shadow of one of the larger islands, he spoke quietly.

"We'll go over now."

"It is still a mile to the Fujiwara island, Commander," the crew chief said.

"We'll have to swim it. According to the chart there's no more cover between here and the island. It's all open water."

"Are there any obstacles we should be aware of?" Siobhan asked the chief, studying the chart herself in the dim cabin light.

"No, it is all clear water. The water is deep in this part of the Ariakeno-umi. Even close to shore you can go down forty feet with no problem."

"Don't wait for us. We'll make our own way back to the dock in Arao," Carter said. "You could be spotted out here."

"Good luck," the crew chief said.

They thanked the chief, slid silently over the side, and began to swim slowly toward the unseen island a mile ahead. The pitch-black night of the rural waterway was on their side. Still a half mile from the island, whose outline they could just make out now against the lighter black of the sky, they submerged and swam on underwater.

Carter was the first to surface not ten yards from the steep and rocky shore of the small island. Siobhan came up silently some twenty feet away. They stroked softly close to the shore until they once more reached the small cove behind its headland. The boat was still there, its engine cold now.

They made their way up the narrow trail to the Japanese-style house on the top of the island where everything could be observed in all directions. No one challenged them and they saw no one. There was no light in the small house now. The two agents circled the house, looking down through the trees on all sides. The house seemed empty. They saw nothing anywhere on the island.

"Do we go inside?" Siobhan asked.

"We go in."

Carter picked the lock on the front door. They left their shoes and air tanks in front, stepped inside, and listened. There was no sound. Each took one of the four rooms. The house was empty.

"Not even Fujiwara himself," Siobhan said.

"But the boat never left the island tonight," Carter said.

"Where are the two who shadowed us?"

"And the boat crew?" Carter added. "And Fujiwara's private army? Where could they hide on an island this size?"

"And where is Fujiwara now?"

Carter heard the small sound and raised his arm in warning inside the dark house. Siobhan heard it a second later.

Somewhere out in the night.

The snap of a twig.

A stone rolling.

The faint rustle of some fallen leaves.

They flattened on either side of a window at the front of the house.

"See anything?"

"No," Siobhan said, "but they're all around the house. The sounds. Back and front."

"Yeah," Carter agreed. "They may not know we're here."

"Wait or go find them?"

"Go find them."

At the front door they went down, opened the door, and crawled out right and left against the dark shadow of the house. Carter had Wilhelmina in his hand. Siobhan held her small Walthar PPK.

The shadowy figure came across the open space toward them. It stood silent and immobile.

"Commanders Carter and O'Neill, I believe," Fujiwara Masashige said in Japanese.

Powerful beams of light came from all directions— from behind the shadowy figure, from either side, from behind Carter and Siobhan and the house. No longer a shadow, Fujiwara Masashige stood in the dazzling spotlights focused only on him, still wearing the sumptuous red *hitatare*. Only now he had a pair of samurai swords thrust into the sash.

"As you can see, you are surrounded," the small man said quietly. "Marksmen have you in their infrared sights at this moment. I assure you that you could not raise your pistols without dying instantly. I would greatly regret such an eventuality." Fujiwara smiled. "Then, I expect you would not want me dead yet anyway. Not before you find out what I am doing, eh?"

"Where have you and your men been?" Carter asked as his eyes searched for a sign of the troops hidden in the night. "We know no one left the island the first time we were here, but we couldn't find anyone but you."

"I could explain, Commander, but I would prefer to show you. If you would lay down your weapons, I will do just that."

The two agents watched the night. Whether Fujiwara's marksmen were out there or not, or good enough to kill them in the dark night or not, they were still surrounded by an enemy they could not see at all. They had little choice.

Carter tossed Wilhelmina out toward Fujiwara and stood up. Siobhan stood beside him and dropped her Walther.

"You show good judgment and great confidence in yourselves," Fujiwara said. "Wait to make your fight tomorrow, eh? We understand each other already."

The black-robed men with the red Fujiwara emblem on their headbands materialized from the night all around Fujiwara. Some were armed with the long Japanese swords, and some carried Soviet AK-47 assault rifles. Fujiwara himself picked up Wilhelmina and the Walthar PPK, and handed them to an assistant.

"Come."

The soldiers closed in all around Carter and Siobhan, and with Fujiwara walking ahead of them, they marched away from the house and the cove below to the far side of the island facing the open Ariakeno-umi. There were no lights and no sign of a trail, but the soldiers and Fujiwara knew exactly where they were going.

At the edge of the dark expanse of water itself, Fujiwara turned to the two agents.

"Your scuba tanks are behind you. Put them on now."

They watched as all the soldiers and Fujiwara himself removed their Japanese robes to reveal wet suits underneath. At a command from Fujiwara, the entire side of the island seemed to swing open showing a concealed cove lined with wooden buildings. The soldiers placed their clothes in the buildings, came out, and one by one they slipped into the water of the cove and vanished into the blackness of the Ariakeno-umi. None of them had air tanks.

"Commander Carter, Commander O'Neill."

Fujiwara Masashige stood at the edge of the water in a wet suit that showed his small, compact body to be a solid mass of powerful muscles. In the wet suit he seemed to move like a shadow, a fluid force.

"You will go now."

Carter and Siobhan entered the water and submerged, the soldiers all around them armed with spear guns, Fujiwara Masashige directly behind them armed with a samurai sword. He handled it like a man who knew how to use it.

They swam in a descending line out into the dark water, small lights on the back of each soldier. They looked like a long string of shining pearls going deeper toward the very center of the Ariakeno-umi.

Then Carter saw it directly ahead: on the bottom some forty feet down was a large transparent dome that seemed to shine with a deep blue light of its own.

EIGHTEEN

"In Japan we have been learning to live on the sea bottom for many years," Fujiwara Masashige said. "This is only a small dome, enough to protect an installation the size of a large house. We are self-contained, create our own air atmosphere, and have our own waste facilities and recycling processes much as does a spaceship."

The small, muscular man sat on the raised platform of a room almost identical to that in his house on the island. Carter and Siobhan sat in the lower area. There were no guards visible, but the two agents knew they were not far away, and Fujiwara could defend himself with his sword until they reached him. They had entered the dome through air locks, and inside there was no sense of being at the bottom of the sea. The air seemed normal, and the light was a pleasant, muted yellow like morning sunlight.

"Why?" Carter said.

Fujiwara was wearing a less formal kimono of dark blue silk and wide silk trousers, two swords thrust into his sash. Carter and Siobhan also wore Japanese clothing, Carter in a similar kimono and trousers, Siobhan in complete female dress with tight sash and obi and narrow skirt that made it difficult to walk. Her eyes were angry as she glared at Fujiwara; he ignored her.

"At first because it was there to do, Commander Carter," Fujiwara said, then smiled again. It was the smile of a man without humor, who only smiled to show his amusement at a world inferior to himself. "Or should I call you Killmaster, agent N3 of AXE, America's most secret espionage agency?"

"Whatever," Carter said. "The installation for underwater living—why now?"

Fujiwara frowned. "You are not surprised I know who you really are? You do not wonder how I know?"

"Surprise is a useless emotion. You know who I am. How is not important right now."

The muscular Japanese nodded. "You are an interesting man, Mr. Carter. I thought you could be from the start."

"The start?" Siobhan said.

Fujiwara did not look at her. "Females do not speak to Fujiwara until they are commanded to speak. You will remember that, Commander O'Neill."

"No, I don't think I will, Mr. Fujiwara, but give me a sword and you'll remember."

The little man looked at her now. "So?"

She looked at him. "Tell us about the start, Mr. Fujiwara."

He nodded slowly, then turned back toward Carter. "From the first time my people encountered you at the Kwajalein reef I have been tracking you."

"And trying to kill us," Carter said.

"You were a danger. But you defeated all our attacks, from the reef to the bomb on the Australian jet. And then the swordsmanship when my men attacked at the Ashekagi house. Remarkable, Mr. Carter. You are a superior man."

"I wasn't alone," Carter said.

"No, you were not." Fujiwara looked again at Siobhan, a certain interest in his dark eyes now, even respect.

She watched him. "You haven't told us why underwater living is so important to you now."

Fujiwara's eyes seemed to blaze up in a sudden surge of fire. He stood on the raised platform and began to pace, his hand on the hilt of his long *katana*.

"At first I thought the only way would be a space vehicle, perhaps one of the moons of Saturn or Jupiter, some giant vehicle we could live on for hundreds of years, a self-contained world—Titan or Triton, a satellite large enough to have an atmosphere to protect against the cosmic rays. But the progress in space travel is so slow, so impossibly slow!"

Fujiwara paced faster, waving his free hand angrily, the right hand white where it gripped the hilt of the *katana* thrust into his sash.

"The only way for what?" Carter said.

Fujiwara didn't seem to hear. "Then I learned of the underwater experiments. I studied the entire concept, worked on improvements myself, until I was able to build this dome large enough to protect a house under the sea, with its own atmosphere, waste recycling, artificial sunlight, food production. I had it built and operating here when Ashekagi told me of the seaweed mutant from the space experiment. I knew then that fate had made me the instrument. Destiny had chosen me, and I was ready!"

"Ready for what?" Carter asked.

Siobhan said nothing. She just watched the intense little man as he paced, talked, gripped the hilt of his sword, waved his free hand in sweeping gestures. Her eyes were almost as intense as Fujiwara's as she watched him.

"To do what I have known for a long time must be done, Killmaster," the fiery Japanese said, turning his dark eyes to stare at Carter. "This world is a sick world, a filthy and evil world. We have lost all that made us human: truth, honor, courage, vision, community, purpose, faith, love. Half the world turns men into cogs, machines, slaves—faceless and without honor or vision as individuals. The other half institutionalizes injustice and corrupts human potential in favor of a code of greed and injustice that has no sense of human community, or love, or personal honor."

He stood on the raised level and stared down at Carter. "We have lost the truth of the past, lost honor for greed, lost vision for safety. Drab slaves or corrupt thieves! We must return to an older, simpler, nobler way of life on this planet, Mr. Carter, or we will vanish in our own corruption, our own lack of vision and purpose. It is time to end this corrupt, purposeless, honorless, lost world we have and begin again. I will wipe the slate clean, start all over, and perhaps this time we can go forward without losing all that is good about us as a species."

Carter looked up at the fierce-eyed man with his old-fashioned kimono and sash full of swords, saw his intense, brilliant, and violent eyes.

"Wipe the slate clean," Carter said slowly, "with incredibly fast-growing, deadly seaweed?"

Fujiwara stood on the low raised section of the room like the statue of an ancient *daimyo*, his head shaved, his hand on his sword. He did not smile now as he looked at Carter and then at Siobhan, who was still watching him intently.

"Yes," Fujiwara said. "With an incredibly fast-growing and deadly seaweed."

"You're crazy," Carter said.

"Perhaps," Fujiwara said, and shrugged. "I must be a little insane or I would not be strong enough to do what must be done—a certain mental state the present society would call insane, but it does not prevent me from knowing what must be done if we are to have any future on this earth as a species. The way we are going we will destroy ourselves in a few centuries, perhaps sooner, and destroy the entire planet with us. My way, we will only cease to exist in our present form sooner, and the planet will not be damaged beyond repair. Perhaps I'm not so insane at that."

"How did you get the seaweed?"

"Dr. Ashekagi was one of my followers. He had been for years. When the NASA experiment resulted in the mutant plant, and he learned what it could do, he informed me. I sensed instantly what I had to do. He gave me the data and some samples, but unfortunately his associates put the weed into the Ariakeno-umi and the government became involved. Dr. Ashekagi realized that he would be questioned, watched, and perhaps would be forced to reveal our plans. He asked to die. We accepted his honorable sacrifice and promised to take complete care of his family, which we have done."

"And now you have the weed and are testing it all over, poisoning the sea," Carter said. "To destroy the world."

Fujiwara's eyes blazed again. "To *save* the world, Killmaster! To destroy the corrupt body of mankind to save the soul of mankind!"

"We don't live in the sea, Fujiwara," Siobhan said suddenly, still without taking her gaze from the small man.

Fujiwara nodded. "No, Commander O'Neill, but the rain does."

"The rain?" Carter said.

"One of the first things Ashekagi told me was that the poison would make the sea deadly, and that would make the rain deadly. And after a few years, perhaps only a year, there would be no life left on this planet. None."

"But not *all* life, Fujiwara," Carter said. "You and your army will be in a dome under the sea. You'll have special wet suits with special breathing apparatus and one-man submarines, and you'll farm and forage on the bottom of the ocean because the poison doesn't affect plant life."

"My people and I, and a group of others I am even now in the process of selecting. You two have impressed me greatly with your intelligence, skill, and sense of honor. Perhaps you would find it possible to join me?"

"And if we don't find it possible?"

Fujiwara shrugged. "To keep you imprisoned would mean far too much risk, and obviously I cannot allow you to leave."

"Obviously," Carter said.

Fujiwara looked at each of them. They said nothing more. Carter stood, his eyes meeting Fujiwara's gaze without flinching. Siobhan remained seated, kneeling, looking up at Fujiwara. The muscular Japanese sighed.

"Perhaps you will think about the possibility. I would be honored to have two so strong and determined with me for the future." He clapped his hands loudly.

"How long under the ocean, Fujiwara?" Carter asked.

"A generation. Perhaps less. Dr. Ashekagi said the poison would slowly dissipate. It would sink into the earth and lose its power in a hundred years. We would not see the surface again except in our protective suits, but the world would be reborn. A clean world. But since then my people have found an antidote to the poison and a chemical that will kill the weed. How long it will take to cleanse the entire earth we do not know, but perhaps we ourselves would see the surface again in our lifetimes."

Four guards in black kimonos entered on Fujiwara's signal. Siobhan stood suddenly.

"I'll do it! I'll join you!"

Fujiwara whirled and strode to her, his hands out in welcome. So fast even Carter barely saw it, so fast Fujiwara stood as if paralyzed, the Australian woman jumped away from the muscular little man, his long *katana* in her hands.

The four guards sprang toward her, drawing their swords.

"Beautiful," Fujiwara said softly as he stared at Siobhan, and he raised his hands to stop the charging guards. He drew his short *wakizashi* and moved in toward Siobhan.

Carter broke the neck of the guard nearest him with a single karate chop, grabbed the long sword from his dead fingers, and dashed out the door the guards had left open. Siobhan had given him his chance; he had to take it no matter what happened to her. Too much was at stake for both their countries.

He found himself in a narrow passage and heard the guards coming out of the room behind him. A metal door straight ahead had a watertight seal, was dogged all around, but the dogs were open. Carter reached the door and spun the hydraulic wheel that opened it. Footsteps pounded behind him.

He whirled, parried the lunging slash of the black-robed guard, and cut deep into the man's neck at the shoulder, blood gushing. The man's sword fell, his eyes glazed with shock, and he collapsed in a pool of his own blood, mortally wounded.

The second guard hesitated.

It cost him his life. The third guard appeared at the far end of the passage and Carter couldn't wait. With a cry, he leaped on the man in front of him, caught his parry, and cut him down in a single unexpected thrust.

Blood still dripping from his sword, Carter was through the door and clanged it closed, dogging it down all around before the last guard could reach it.

He was in a narrow stairwell that spiraled upward to the curved translucent skin of the dome. The dogs were already opening again on the door from the other side. He ran up the spiral stairs and at the top found an escape air lock. By the time he got it open and closed, the chamber filled with water and the outer door opened, Fujiwara's men would be there to reopen the inner door and drag him out.

He could hear them below. Fujiwara's own voice echoed somewhere in the distance along the passage he had left.

Carter took the long *katana* in both hands and hacked the thick plastic skin of the dome. He slashed at it again and again. The razor-sharp, unbreakable steel plunged through. A small stream of water spurted in. Carter punched two more holes as he heard them start up the stairs. A long crack appeared between two of the holes, the plastic bending now under the weight of the water, and a large chunk broke away sending a torrent of water to the bottom of the stairwell.

Below he heard Fujiwara ordering them out. They would have to close off the stairwell to prevent the dome from flooding.

He had maybe a two-minute advantage before Fujiwara could send his men to other air locks.

Carter crawled into the air lock and closed the small inner door. He opened the valves and waited for the chamber to fill before he could open the outer door. A small air pocket remained when the pressure was equal enough for him to force the outer door open. Carter took a deep breath, swam out, and kicked for the surface.

He broke through into the dark night and swam hard for Fujiwara Masashige's small island. They would be after him in minutes. But the last place they would look would be Fujiwara's own island.

He was ashore and moving up the slope toward the small Japanese house when he heard them breaking the surface out in the Ariakeno-umi. Voices called in Japanese, instructing them to spread out and swim in all directions. Flashlights went on all across the dark waterway. One voice instructed some to swim for the island and get the boat.

Carter ran silently on up to the dark house.

Inside he found the telephone and dialed the secret code of numbers that connected him to the AXE computer. The series of clicks and pings and bleeps was longer than usual. A rural connection.

"Hello there, N3, are you—" the soft, sultry voice began.

Carter punched in the automatic six-digit code for extreme emergency rescue, gave his coordinates and the verbal instructions, "Fujiwara island in Ariakeno-umi, immediate," and slipped back out into the night and the trees.

Four shapes in wet suits jogged up to the house and entered warily, searching.

"Empty. He was not so clever."

They ran back down toward the shore.

Among the trees Carter waited. He looked at his watch, all that Fujiwara had left him of his equipment. A minute had passed.

Two minutes.

The boat started down in the cove, backed out, and began to make long sweeps around the island, its searchlight picking out the heads of the swimming troops of Fujiwara Masashige.

Five minutes.

Voices came up the slopes of the island again toward the house. Someone had begun to wonder about the island.

Carter heard the sound to the east.

Two jets were coming in fast. Lights swept low over the water and the island, illuminating the boat and the swimming heads. Machine guns and small cannon fired as the jets roared over, banked, and swung back to sweep in again. The swimmers dived, and the boat twisted in evasive maneuvers. On the island the voices froze among the trees as the jets swept in once more.

And again.

The roar of the jet engines filled the sky.

Carter didn't hear the helicopter until it was hovering almost directly over the small house.

The Killmaster ran for the dangling harness, caught it, and the chopper vanished into the dark night before anyone on the island or in the Ariakeno-umi knew there had even been a helicopter.

As the American Army crew leaned over and cranked him up, Carter looked at his watch again. It had been ten minutes since he had made his call to Washington. AXE was getting slow.

NINETEEN

The boats of the Japanese defense force ringed the area on the surface of the Ariakeno-umi above the submerged dome. On the deck of the command boat, Nick Carter stood with David Hawk himself.

"Blown up, flooded, and everyone gone," Carter said. "The three bodies of the men I killed, no one else. Not even Siobhan."

Hawk smoked and chewed one of his cheap cigars. Carter stood in a wet suit and scuba gear, his mask up now, water dripping from him. The rest of the divers still searched the surface and the depths for any trace of survivors or bodies. Hawk stared grimly down at the dark water off the small island where other soldiers of the defense force combed the woods for signs of Fujiwara and his men.

"She sacrificed herself so I could escape," Carter said.

"It's in the report," Hawk said gruffly. "She could be alive. We haven't found her body. Where the hell are they, Nick?"

"Anywhere."

"Three hours, that's all they had, and the jets were coming over regularly. Where are they and how did they get away without anyone seeing a hair of them?"

"Underwater," Carter said. "Fujiwara plans to live under the ocean for a hundred years at least, and if he was testing the weed in the open, he was ready. He would have been prepared for underwater escape with those special tankless suits that must make their own oxygen from chemicals that react with seawater, one-man submarines, or the large submersibles. And somewhere he's got a dome big enough for his army and then some."

"Where?"

"I've got a hunch. Get me a new set of my equipment and a couple of special items."

"You'll go alone?"

"Fujiwara's got Siobhan."

"Not good enough, Nick. We've got to stop him; she's expendable."

"We need Fujiwara alive with the antidote to the poison and the weed killer. He'd kill himself and all of them, and leave the weed to grow and destroy us. He'd rather see us all end than go on the way we are."

Hawk chewed on the foul cigar. "Where?" he growled.

"Off Kwajalein, where that Soviet ship was destroyed. It's the only logical answer. The Russians were too close to his big dome."

"Let's get your equipment."

It was just after dawn when Nick Carter's fighter jet swept in low over the giant lagoon and touched down on the airfield of Kwajalein. He had seen the black water as he passed over the lagoon. The weed filled it now shore to shore, the shoots moving like the heads of a million snakes.

General Scott was waiting on the airstrip, wearing his pistols, with an armed squad of his men. He was tight-lipped, but there was a glint in his eyes.

"I have instructions to place my entire command under your orders," the ramrod-straight little general said. He was angry at being upstaged but excited by the prospect of action.

"No orders," Carter said, "just some help, General."

The general looked happier. "That's what I'm here for. What do you need?"

"A boat and crew, full scuba gear, spear gun, four extra air tanks, and an underwater sled for carrying the tanks."

"Men?"

"No."

The general was disappointed. There wasn't much action for him in supplying Carter with equipment.

"An armed guard on the boat, perhaps. It might be good if you were out there to back me up, General."

The general beamed. Carter suppressed a smile.

"Let's get you going," the general said.

They left the field with the armed escort, the general leading as if on a forced march to catch the enemy by surprise. At the headquarters building Major Hammond took the list of what Carter needed, then the general went to work getting the boat ready, and Carter went to his old quarters to prepare his own equipment. A new Luger took Wilhelmina's place, a new Pierre was strapped to his upper thigh, and a new Hugo went up his sleeve under the wet suit.

He slipped his emergency equipment inside his waterproof container and strapped on the heavy waterproof diving watch with its hidden devices. He took a tight roll of what looked like some thin cloth Hawk had brought him, wrapped it almost flat around his waist, then wrapped a smaller piece around his thigh under Pierre. He put on a suit of silk thermal underwear to wear under the wet suit. Fujiwara hadn't searched him in the Ariakeno-umi dome; he had simply taken everything including the wet suit but not his long underwear or watch.

He was in his wet suit and ready when the firing erupted in the direction of the headquarters building.

Heavy firing. Uzis and AK-47s and M-16s from the sounds. Grenades. Rocket launchers.

Carter drew his Lugar and ran toward the sound of the firing.

They were everywhere.

Men in black wet suits with built-in masks and without air tanks swarmed over the grounds. Small helicopters hovered, firing down at the buildings and the fleeing American civilians.

Carter ran for the headquarters building. Five of the attackers saw him. He shot down three before they could even yell. The other two dived for cover. Carter didn't wait; he ran on and into the headquarters building. Major Hammond was dead across his desk, his pistol still in its holster. Soldiers lay in the corridors in their blood.

The master sergeant slumped dead outside General Scott's office. Inside, the office was empty, the windows smashed, the walls riddled with bullets. Two dead attackers in their wet suits without tanks lay on the floor.

Carter heard firing close by. He dropped, crawled to the shattered windows, and peered out. Twenty yards across the lawn behind the headquarters building ten American soldiers were making a stand behind an old World War II Japanese bunker, General Scott clear among them, shouting defiance.

The black-suited attackers were closing a ring around them but had not yet completed the encirclement. The reason became clear: three mortar shells exploded among the black-garbed attackers attempting to close the circle, sending them diving back for cover.

It was the general himself aiming the three mortars, slapping the shoulders of the prone loaders to fire one after the other. And the general had chosen his ground well. The half-destroyed bunker gave cover in front, a high earth bank protected sides and rear, and a thick grove of palms around the entire area prevented the small helicopter gunships from getting close enough to fire straight down.

But they were closing the circle and would overwhelm the position as soon as the general ran out of mortar shells. The general needed a diversion, a crossfire to break up the line of the attackers.

Carter crawled back out into the corridor and ran for the armory at the far end. Other dead soldiers lay in the corridor, but the attackers had gone on. In the armory he found what he needed—an XM-174 automatic grenade launcher with four fully-loaded twelve-round magazines in a canvas carrying sling. Carter unlocked it from its tripod mount and ran back down the corridor to the general's office.

The firing was still heavy outside.

Carter crawled back to the window dragging the XM-174 and the sling of ammo. He raised up and peered out again. The circle had been closed, and there were fewer men kneeling behind the old blockhouse with the general and the three mortars. It wouldn't be long.

Carter raised up on one knee, rested the automatic grenade launcher on the windowsill, locked on a magazine, set the gun on semiautomatic, and aimed for the line of black-suited attackers between him and the window.

He fired.

Moved the sights left. Fired.

Moved the sights right. Fired.

The three spin-stabilized grenades exploded among the attackers one after the other in a rapid-fire line.

Carter aimed over the blockhouse and the general's beleaguered troops at the attackers on the far side, and fired another three grenades.

Then he fired one right and one left.

The remaining four he fired again at the attackers closest to him, then he pulled off the magazine and slammed home a second magazine.

The surviving attackers broke and ran for the cover of the other buildings. The general hurried them on their way with three more mortar shells.

Carter heard someone running into the headquarters

building, dropped the grenade launcher, and whirled with his Lugar pointing at the office door.

She came in running, breathing hard, her hair disheveled.

He had to jerk his hand left to miss her as he shot.

Siobhan!

"Nick! Christ, it's me!"

She carried a short M-16Al and dived to the floor behind a chair as Carter shot before he could stop.

"How?" Carter said, crawling to her.

"Fujiwara brought me with them and left a guard on me. I slipped him in the fight."

"The general's out there with a few men. I've cleared out Fujiwara's troops for a moment with a grenade launcher, but they'll be back, and I think the general's people are all the resistance left." He listened, but there was no sound of firing from anywhere else across the island and its Midwestern suburban village. "Cover my rear."

He crawled back to the window, picked up the grenade launcher, and peered out again. Fujiwara's men were creeping back as the sun beat down on the few American soldiers left behind the old bunker around the general. Even as Carter watched, he saw the general fire his last mortar shell, pat his men on the back, and take out his pistols.

"It's up to us," Carter said over his shoulder, and raised the grenade launcher to the windowsill.

The burst of automatic fire from behind him knocked the launcher from his hands.

The Killmaster whirled, reaching for Wilhelmina.

Siobhan O'Neill shot him in the right arm.

"Sorry," she said. "You're not an easy man to argue with. Just don't make any moves, Nick."

Four of Fujiwara's men came into the room behind her.

Carter turned and looked back out the window.

The attackers were all standing now, covering the window. Behind the bunker, the general and his last few men stood with their hands up. Carter turned back to Siobhan, who held her stubby M-16A1 pointed at his heart.

"Nice work," the Killmaster said.

She waved the commando gun. "Take him. Get his air tanks and bring him to the boat." She looked at Carter. "Be very careful—he's tough and tricky. Tie him up—hold him on ropes. Keep two men ten feet behind all the time. Keep your guns out and your eyes on him. All of you."

Carter smiled. "I sound like a one-man army."

Siobhan said nothing, and walked out of the general's shattered office. Three men tied Carter's arms tight to his body Japanese style, attached ropes to his wrists, and stepped back. They dragged him up and pulled him out of the office along the corridor and out into the hot morning sun of Kwajalein.

The peaceful island was a shambles now, the black-kimono-clad soldiers of Fujiwara everywhere, rounding up the Americans. They pulled Carter to the ocean-side beach and shoved him aboard a large rubber boat. Six men paddled the giant raft out through the reef breakers to where the large submersible waited heaving ponderously on the Pacific swells. Carter was pushed and pulled aboard, then shoved down a hatch into the interior of the submersible. He heard the hatch close and felt the undersea craft move into a dive.

"Forward."

He walked forward to a low room with the row of small windows open to the clear undersea world as they descended. Siobhan sat there alone, her M-16A1 on her lap. They pushed Carter into a chair, and four of them stood around the room behind him with their weapons ready. Siobhan did not offer to untie him. She wore Japanese dress, female dress, but she had a pair of swords thrust into the sash like a samurai.

"How long?" Carter asked the Australian woman.

"Only yesterday."

"Why?"

She shrugged. "I like his ideas. I've had the same thoughts. I like him. He's even stronger than you, Nick. I've looked for a man like him for a long time."

"The world?"

"It won't be missed."

"Me?"

She smiled. "We'll talk." And she suddenly leaned forward. "There it is!"

Through the row of narrow windows he saw a deep blue glow that seemed to fill the entire bottom of the sea. A gigantic plastic dome covered the flat top of an undersea mountain some thousand feet below the surface, a dome large enough to cover a city. Torpedolike one-man submarines came and went through air locks, and their submersible was heading straight toward it.

TWENTY

Carter sat in the narrow, windowless, bare room. Stripped to his underwear, he sat on tatami mats and leaned against the smooth plastic of the wall.

The air had that stale, chemical quality of windowless vaults deep beneath a city.

The light came from nowhere, diffused and cold.

He was surrounded by total, oppressive silence.

There was nothing alive except himself, and how long would that be?

Imprisoned in the narrow, low-ceilinged room, Carter listened for voices but heard none. He thought about a hundred years in the plastic air and light deep under the sea with nowhere to go. Nothing but exercises and games and training and libraries, and occasional swims out to tend the crops and harvest the shellfish and fish to feed the submerged survivors who could wait down here a hundred years.

Could they do it?

Maybe the Japanese could do it better than any other people. After all, they had spent 250 years in an artificial world under a plastic dome of ruthless self-isolation. It was possible. He didn't think he could do it, but maybe they could if anyone could.

He began to study the narrow cell. It was not much bigger than a box, too low for a man his size to stand up in. The walls and floor and ceiling were all smooth plastic. The door was the full width of the room, and would open outward. There was nowhere to hide and jump someone coming in. No crevices or protrusions. No sink or toilet.

No way out. Only there always was. The air had to come from somewhere. And the light. Behind the apparent smooth plastic there had to be vents, electrical connections, conduits. There was no such thing as a sealed room beyond the tomb.

He was still searching for a flaw when they came for him.

"Come."

They stood in the open doorway dressed in the usual black robes but now with beautiful *jimbaori* jackets embroidered with the Fujiwara crest over the dark kimonos. They were somehow more confident and more relaxed at the same time. In the clan stronghold. At home.

Carter bent to go out into the narrow passage. The leader of the guards handed him a black kimono to put over his underwear, a pair of sandals, and a sash. Dressed, Carter was marched along the passage toward a watertight door.

Voices came to meet him, voices everywhere through the steel watertight door. From above, from below. Crowds of voices talking, shouting in team games, drilling and shouting. Voices and the pounding of feet, the clash of wooden kendo swords, the ringing steel of real samurai swords in close-combat training.

The guards took him through the steel door into a much larger corridor filled with people in black kimonos hurrying along, moving in and out of rooms on either side. Through another door they crossed a large public room where kendo classes were in session, karate classes, and plain exercise classes.

There were two more large rooms filled with games,

conferences, and every kind of group activity before
Carter was taken into a Japanese-style waiting room.
Each room in the underwater complex was protected
with watertight doors, all apparently made to look like
rooms familiar to those who would live in the dome.
The domed installation was as large as a small town,
and was probably able to sustain a thousand people or
more.

A tall black in a sumptuous red *hitatare* slid open a
door and motioned to Carter like a major-domo. The
guards went in with Carter this time. Fujiwara learned
quickly, or perhaps Siobhan had reminded them of the
Killmaster's skills.

They sat together on the raised *jodan no ma*. Siobhan
wore voluminous red robes embroidered in gold over a
white underskirt. She wore all female attire—except for
the swords thrust into the sash. Fujiwara was in a simple
off-white *noshi* jacket from the twelfth century over
plain white *hakama* trousers, showing in stark contrast
the pair of black lacquered and gold-fitted swords in the
white sash.

The tall black motioned for Carter to sit on a cushion
on the mats facing the raised platform. A small table
stood in front of the cushion, holding a white porcelain
sake decanter and a single white cup. The sake was just
warm. A single rose in a dark blue bud vase decorated
the table.

"A daring and resourceful escape, Killmaster," Fujiwara said solemnly, "but this time we are much too far
down. The pressure alone would kill you before you
could get halfway up."

"I couldn't have escaped at all without Siobhan,"
Carter said with a smile.

"No," the Australian said, "you couldn't have."

"It is one of the things I most admired about her,"
Fujiwara said. "A rare woman. I did not believe such a
woman existed. One is always learning in life."

"Yes," Carter said, looking at Siobhan. "Only since
yesterday, Commander?"

"Only then for Masashige," Siobhan said, "perhaps all my life for someone like him. You're a powerful man, Nick, but you lack vision, the vision that brings greatness."

"Vision or insanity?" Carter mused.

"Sometimes they can be quite close," Siobhan said, and smiled at Fujiwara. "You have to really know someone before you can tell the difference."

"Sometimes not even then," Carter said.

Fujiwara's eyes darkened, and his hand touched the hilt of his *katana*. Siobhan put her hand on his arm. The muscular Japanese took a deep breath.

"Please, Killmaster, the sake is for your comfort as we talk," he said.

Carter poured a cup. "Talk about what?"

"Your future," Fujiwara said.

"And the future of the world," Siobhan added.

The sake was excellent. Carter sipped, savored, and waited. Maybe Fujiwara thought he could use Carter, or maybe it was Siobhan's conscience, but they didn't want to kill him. It was what he had counted on, his one big advantage, and he had to use it somehow to destroy Fujiwara and his insane plan. How would depend on what they did, what they had brought him here to talk about. So he sipped the warm rice wine, smiled, and waited.

"The world as we know it will end, Nick," Siobhan said. "The people. Only we in this dome will be left. We want the survivors, those who will start a new world, to be the best. We want you, Nick."

"Is that it?" Carter said. "You're that afraid to die?"

Fujiwara clutched the hilt of his sword again, and half rose on the raised platform.

"No," Siobhan said. "He is probing for weakness, Masashige. Let me go on."

"Why do we need him, lady? We should kill him now!"

"We need his skills, his brain, his knowledge,

Masashige. We will need a man like him when we emerge." She looked down at Carter. "Him or his children."

Carter watched her, and sipped the warm sake.

"Join us, Nick. We have a woman for you, a place. You can take the place of the man who killed himself in the Ashekagis' courtyard. He was Masashige's closest associate. You can be that to us."

"And if not?"

Fujiwara spoke. "You will die with the rest of the corrupt animals of this earth of ours."

"And when will that be, Fujiwara? Even the seaweed will take years, maybe decades to fill the oceans."

Fujiwara smiled. "No, it will not be that long, Killmaster. My scientists have developed an even newer strain of the mutant, and this very day it will go on its mission to every corner of the earth. Perhaps a month, a week, and the rain will fall to end the eons of corruption."

"Don't tell him," Siobhan said.

"Why? He will not escape from here," Fujiwara said.

"If we don't tell him, it won't matter even if he does," she said.

Fujiwara nodded slowly. Carter sipped his sake. Fujiwara had already told him enough. All he had to do was escape.

"Well, Carter?" Fujiwara said. "What will it be? Death, or life with us down here and a new future for mankind?"

"Doesn't sound like I have much choice," Carter said. "There's no way out of here, so even if I don't agree with anything you say or do, it looks like I'll be here or dead. On the whole, I'd rather hang around and see what I can do to help the new world. With you two making it, it may need a lot of help."

Fujiwara frowned. "Does that mean yes or no?"

"It means I think you're both crazy, but it looks like I'm going to be with you after everyone else is dead whether I want to or not. It means you can't ever go

back, Fujiwara; nothing can ever be erased, and those
good old days of yours weren't that good anyway. The
truth is, we're better today than we ever were; we just
have a way to go to be really good. Maybe a long way. It
means I guess I'm with you down here, and there's not
much I can do about it, so I might as well join you. I
hope that woman you've got for me is good-looking and
sexy as hell. It's going to be a long fifty or so years down
here."

Siobhan laughed. "You're a wonder, Nick Carter.
Don't believe a word of that, Masashige. He doesn't.
He's just playing us for time."

"Of course, my lady, but he may be a lot more right
than he thinks. So we'll hold him, and after we've
cleaned up the rest of the world, we can talk to him
again. Is that agreeable to you?"

Siobhan hesitated. "Perhaps you're right, Masashige.
We should kill him, and now."

"Perhaps," Fujiwara said. "But, like you, lady, I
hate to waste such a man if we can have him with us
later. Who knows what may happen on the surface
while we wait, or what we will find when we emerge. We
will keep him in that cell, and watch him until it is over
on the surface." Fujiwara nodded to the guards. "Take
him back."

Carter finished his sake, smiled at Siobhan, and stood
up. The guards closed around him and they marched
out. Despite Siobhan, Fujiwara had told him enough.
Whatever they were going to do would require action
that could not happen there in the dome a thousand feet
under the ocean, and was going to happen soon,
perhaps within hours. It meant they would be leaving
the dome to go somewhere, and it meant that they
would all be very busy.

Too busy to worry about one man locked safely in a
two-by-four solid cell.

He was marched back through the large public rooms
where he saw that the soldiers seemed to be preparing
for something, sharpening their swords and cleaning

their rifles, the officers conferring. Along the corridors everyone was busy now in the offices. In his passage only one guard watched the door of his cell as they pushed him back in once more.

He waited only until he heard the clang of the steel door behind the men who had brought him, and then, alone on the floor of the narrow little room, Carter went to work.

He quickly stripped off his silk long johns and unwrapped the all-but-invisible body wrap he'd had prepared for just this kind of emergency. Laid out on the floor it was a complete bodysuit of an ultralight, ultrastrong, ultrainsulated plastic fabric, complete with a clear eye piece and an exhaling valve.

He listened at the door, but there was no sound out in the narrow passage except the distant breathing of the single guard, alone and bored, as sure as Fujiwara that there was nowhere for the prisoner to escape to even if he could get out of the cell.

Back at the spread-out suit, he took off his watch, opened the back, and took out a miniature valve no bigger than his smallest fingernail. He attached the tiny valve to the suit, and listened again. No one moved in the passage.

He unwrapped a long flat rectangle of the same ultrastrong plastic fabric from his leg and attached it to the other end of the miniature valve. Then he dressed in his underwear again, and slowly, carefully, slipped into the thin bodysuit, drew it up as far as his neck, and listened once more.

Satisfied there was no one in the passage but the single guard, Carter opened the thick strap of the watch in three places, opened the back of the watch again, and took out the quartz battery. When he had assembled the four pieces and the miniature battery, he had an L-shaped instrument that rested easily in the palm of his hand. Holding it between thumb and forefinger by the short arm of the L, he carefully studied the door and measured up from the floor until he was sure of exactly where the lock and knob were.

He aimed the long arm of the L, and a narrow laser beam bit deeply into the smooth plastic of the door. The laser cut through the plastic like butter, swiftly and silently. He had almost cut the large square through when he became aware of an odor. . . .

The plastic was giving off a gas that had a strong, pungent odor.

Outside, the guard moved. Steps came slowly toward the door. Carter could picture the guard's face, his nose sniffing, his eyes questioning as he came along the passage looking for the source of the stink. Not alarmed yet, only puzzled. Not sure just where the odor was coming from. Bending and sniffing as he moved to the door. At the door he'd blink, perhaps see the faint outline of the laser cut. Bend closer to see what it could be. . . .

Carter hurled his weight against the door, knowing it opened outward so a prisoner could not hide behind it. It burst open leaving the square of plastic with the lock still firmly attached to the doorframe. The guard was hurled across the narrow passage to smash against the wall and bounce off into Carter's deadly karate slash at his neck.

The neck snapped with a sickening crack of bone, and the man's dead body dropped limp to the floor.

Carter dragged the body inside the cell and stripped it, then he put on the black kimono and sandals. The guard had no keys. Carter closed the door around the cut-out square, picked up the guard's AK-47, and ran lightly to the door at the end of the passage. He listened. People moved beyond the door, hurrying along the wider corridor as if in the last stages of preparation for the mission. There was no lessening of the traffic, and the Killmaster couldn't wait.

He used his tiny laser gun on the visible lock, burning through the steel bolt this time, and opened the door.

People passed, but no one even glanced at him as he stepped out with his Kalishnikov and closed the door.

They should have known that the guard could not let himself out, but they didn't think about it, busy with their own assignments.

He moved quickly along the broad corridor as if on some vital mission. His eyes searched for what he needed: the air lock entry from the submersible. They should be loading the underwater craft, getting ready to leave, taking . . . and he saw them: four men in white coats escorting a cart loaded with large metal containers.

Carter followed among the hurrying Fujiwara soldiers.

The room they walked into had an extrathick watertight door, and they had to lift the cart over the watertight lip at the bottom. The small room had a heavy hatch-door already open on the far side that led to another open doorway and the inside of the submersible where Fujiwara himself was supervising preparations. The powerful little Japanese looked at his watch and urged his men to move faster in the work of loading the submersible.

Carter went on past. They would be leaving soon . . . to wherever they were going.

It took him ten more minutes to find the air locks where the one-man submarines entered the dome. Everyone was involved with the imminent trip of the submersible, and the smaller air lock room was empty. Carter slipped quickly inside one of the air locks, closed the inner hatch, and took off his watch one last time. This time he screwed the entire watch to the tiny valve, then opened the sea valves to let the air lock flood.

When the chamber was half full, he slipped the last piece of the thin plastic suit over his head, closed the steel zipper, and submerged. Almost instantly the cloth rectangle attached to the tiny valve inflated as pure oxygen poured from the watch when the chemicals embedded inside reacted with the seawater. Carter opened the valve into the plastic suit as the water filled the chamber. The pressure equalized as Carter breathed slowly, opened the outer hatch, and swam out into the sea beside the dome.

Protected by his plastic pressure suit, breathing the oxygen that gave both the pressure and his air, he swam through the deep water illuminated only by the dark blue glow of the dome itself until he reached the submersible fastened to the dome through its air lock. He kicked up to the conning tower and grabbed the handholds set into the deck for holding on to when the submersible was on the surface in rough weather.

He waited.

They would find the dead guard sooner or later, and they would search the dome from top to bottom looking for him in a black kimono. They would search the submersible. They would not find him. No one would even imagine he had left the dome at this depth. Except, perhaps, Siobhan, and even she would not imagine he had a pressure suit for the deep water, so they would go on looking. When they were sure he was not on the submersible, they would leave on their mission.

The only problem was how much time he had before the submersible left for whatever its destination was. His air would only last a few hours.

Before he even finished the thought he heard the heavy hatch doors close and felt the sub begin to shiver as its engines took hold. It moved, starting upward to its final destination, carrying its terrible cargo.

Carter held tight as they rode upward. He had no problem now, except, somehow, to stop them from destroying the world.

TWENTY-ONE

The sea remained dark until a faint silver tinged the surface above, and the bottom was suddenly shallower. It was night, a moonlit night, and Nick Carter knew where the submersible and Fujiwara were going. Back to Kwajalein. There was no other atoll close to the underwater city.

When he saw the reef dim ahead, and felt the submersible begin to rise toward the surface, he released his hold and let himself drift back until he was clear of the propellors. Then he turned and swam over the reef and into the shallows around the string of tiny islands.

Only when he was almost onshore did he cautiously surface, unzip the thin suit, and pull back the headpiece. He looked carefully all around. In the distance in the moonlight the submersible was on the surface, unmoving, floodlights on and figures filling its decks, rubber boats being slid over the sides to cross the reef and land on the beaches of Kwajalein Island.

Carter waded ashore, removed the collapsible air tank but not the sleek fabric suit, and began to trot toward the dark streets of Kwajalein village. He was on the edge of another of the nine-hole golf courses when he saw the missiles giant in the night. There were six of them—

long-range ICBMs on mobile launchers.

Fujiwara was going to launch his deadly mutant to all corners of the Pacific and Indian oceans in the nose cones of the missiles!

When?

Carter looked up at the moon. It was already late in the night. Fujiwara would want to be off the island as soon as possible to minimize the chance of accidental discovery by some wandering aircraft that could warn the superpowers perhaps in time for them to destroy the missiles in flight.

It meant that Fujiwara would be on full radar alert, and would probably fire at dawn.

It also meant that he did not have much time.

Hawk was standing on alert with an American carrier task force somewhere off the Marshalls far out of radar range. But would there be time for the carrier jets to reach Kwajalein before Fujiwara could fire? Carter didn't know, couldn't risk it. He would activate the signal embedded under his skin when he was sure the missiles could not be launched the instant Fujiwara picked up the jets on radar. Until then, there was only himself and his skill, training, and wits.

He moved on cautiously, crossing the open areas of the golf course toward the buildings on the far side, working his way through the dark, silent, deserted streets toward the main radar tracking installation and the missile launching control center.

The island still looked like some peaceful American village, but a village without people—the way American towns were going to look after the rockets took their mutant cargo to the corners of the earth and the deadly rain began to fall, the way the world would look if Fujiwara wasn't stopped.

Silent, empty houses. Deserted yards and lawns. Abandoned cars, bicycles, children's yard toys.

Where were they? The people?

Had Fujiwara killed them all with the general and his soldiers? No. Fujiwara was insane, but he wasn't a murderer. He would kill for his cause—destroy humanity—but he would not kill innocent people. He would try to recruit them for the dome, or let them go their way and die later under his deadly rain.

Where were they?

Carter turned and began to trot among the empty houses toward the high school. There was only one place Fujiwara's men would imprison captives: the high school gym or swimming pool. As he neared the high school he began to see the black kimonos of the invaders.

They were moving around the high school and the distant radar control center. The ICBMs themselves towered in the night along the main road on their mobile launchers.

At the high school, guards held positions at all the doors and out among the trees, ringing the building. The outdoor pool was not being guarded. As Carter had expected, any prisoners were in the high school gym.

The island motor pool was between the high school and General Scott's headquarters building. Carter moved in a circle among the trees. He needed cover. At the corner of an outbuilding a single soldier wearing a wide Japanese straw hat relieved himself behind some bushes. Carter's arm locked around his throat cutting off any sound.

When the man was dead, Carter stripped his body, hid it in the bushes, dressed again in the black kimono, pulled the wide hat low over his face, and walked out and on toward the motor pool with the soldier's M-16 at the ready. The motor pool was deserted; no one had any need for vehicles on the island this night.

In the dispatcher's building the keys were all neat on their rack of hooks. He took the keys to a six-wheeler and a smaller ammunition carrier, and found a book of matches in the desk drawer. Outside, the moon was almost down, dawn not far away.

Moving like a shadow, Carter filled gasoline cans at the motor pool pump and piled them into the back of the six-wheeler. When it was loaded, he slipped through the night, evading the few soldiers moving on missions or yawning on guard at the buildings, until he reached the headquarters building. It was riddled with bullet holes and grenade damage. There was no guard and it appeared deserted.

Inside, he listened. There was no sound in the shattered, empty corridors. The bodies had been removed, but the blood still stained the floors and walls. He found the armory. The heavy arms had been taken, but the M-16s were still there with their boxes of loaded clips.

Carter took as many as he could carry and worked his way back to the motor pool. He loaded the rifles into the smaller ammo carrier and made two more trips to the armory. As he returned with his last load, the moon was down, the heavy darkness pitch-black toward dawn. But Carter was ready.

He took a bayonet he had picked up in the armory and sliced a thin layer of skin from his left arm exposing a plastic disk. He scratched the disk, activating an electronic signal that would be picked up by AXE receivers everywhere in the world. Hawk would know the location of transmission. The planes from the carrier task force would be at Kwajalein within two hours, maybe less.

And the island radar would pick up the carrier jets within twenty minutes or less.

Carter opened a can of gasoline in the back of the six-wheeler, spilled it all around the other cans, climbed into the cab, and drove slowly toward the missile control center. He saw the shadows of the guards ringed around the building. This was where Fujiwara and Siobhan would be. Here the guards would be alert.

He drove slowly until he saw the gleam of an eye where a tall black figure stood outside the control center. "Where are you going?" came the gruff challenge in Japanese.

The truck had been spotted.

"Launcher parts, emergency," Carter growled in

Japanese, then he stamped hard on the accelerator, tossed a lighted match into the rear, and jumped.

The truck burst into flames, careened straight toward the control building, and exploded in a great roar of fire as it smashed into the wall.

Carter raced back through the night to the motor pool.

The guards from the high school came running toward the explosion. Carter urged them on in excited Japanese.

"Attackers! Everyone to the control center!"

He climbed into the ammunition carrier and drove straight to the high school. The remaining guards were all staring toward the flames that burned at the missile control center. Carter never slowed down. He rammed the ammunition carrier through the side double doors of the gymnasium and skidded to a stop among the startled Americans, the fiesty General Scott himself standing in front of them.

"Carter!"

The Killmaster leaped out.

"In the truck! Guns! All loaded!"

He dropped to the floor with his own M-16 and shot down two black-kimono-clad guards who ran into the gymnasium. The general wasted no time. With the other six soldiers in the big room, he jumped into the truck and started throwing out the rifles.

Carter shot down three more guards.

Two Americans fell, hit by fire from the guards.

The general himself was already prone and firing. The six soldiers were soon covering other doors and windows. The civilians hesitated.

"Take guns!" the general shouted. "Everyone! They can't let us escape now. Fight back!"

Two civilians grabbed rifles. Then four more. Then all of them, men and women. The children were in a far corner. Six of the men ran to protect them.

Suddenly there were no more guards.

"Outside!" Carter cried.

They poured through the double doors and spread out. The general formed them into seven groups, each led by a soldier, and sent them to take up positions in the predawn darkness. He knew the base, knew every good defensive position. On the east a faint line of light tinged the sky over the Pacific.

"General, I have to get to the missile control. Hold all the guards you can as long as you can. Help will be coming in an hour!"

"Good luck, Carter!"

"You too, sir," Carter said. He saluted, turned, and ran off once more.

Still in his black kimono, he went unnoticed in the melee of confused Fujiwara soldiers. Officers bawled orders, but none of them seemed to be sure which way to attack—the gymnasium and the escaped prisoners, or the control center and the flames.

Carter reached the control center. The fire was blazing, but most of it was the truck itself and the cans of gasoline that were still exploding.

A single guard at one door tried to halt Carter, and died in a burst of his own blood.

Another appeared. Carter fired. The M-16 jammed. The guard shot a searing pain through his left hip. Cursing the Pentagon idiots who had ruined the design of the weapon, Carter slammed into the man before he could get off a second shot and heard the neck bone snap as his hands twisted.

Carter grabbed the pair of swords from the sash of the dead guard, ran down the corridor, and burst through the door into the control room.

Fujiwara Masashige stood alone at the missile firing keys and whirled when he heard Carter. He stared.

"So? You have a hundred lives, Killmaster. I would not have believed it. But you are too late. The countdown cannot be stopped now."

"It can be stopped," Carter said.

Fujiwara smiled. He wore now a complete suit of *gusoku*-style Japanese armor, the Fujiwara crest on the helmet. "Only if you come past me. It is too late, Killmaster."

"No," Carter said, and he drew the *katana* and *wakizashi* from his sash.

The door burst open again, and Siobhan ran into the room. Dressed in the same *gusoku*-style light armor, she cried, "Jets coming in on the radar! I knew Carter would bring trouble somehow!" She saw him and froze momentarily, then drew her sword. "Damn you, this time I'll make sure!"

Carter backed against the door and turned the lock.

"Just the three of us," Carter said.

Fujiwara nodded. "With swords, Killmaster? We in armor?"

"Piece of cake." Carter grinned. "Old Australian saying."

Fujiwara's face darkened in anger. Siobhan moved toward Carter.

"This time it's not your cake."

"Woman!" Fujiwara thundered. The muscular Japanese drew his swords. "You go too far! This is for me!"

He moved in toward Carter, *katana* up on his shoulder, *wakizashi* held horizontal in front, feet sliding, knees flexed and loose. Carter waited, both swords at his sides.

Fujiwara darted in, *katana* slashing down, *wakizashi* slicing up and out.

Carter parried the slash, ducked away from the cut, and lunged with his *wakizashi*.

Fujiwara whirled away, came back with a lightning cut of the long sword, and parried Carter's riposte with the short one. Carter caught the cut and stabbed in with the short sword. Both swept past each other, faced, swords up, breathing hard.

Fujiwara leaped in again.

Carter evaded, parried.

Fujiwara pressed in and in.

The fight went on, circling, lunging, as Siobhan

watched with her long sword out, waiting.

She watched, waited.

The sun was up now outside and the countdown for the launch was almost ended. The two men were almost perfectly matched, Fujiwara with the edge of the armor. Siobhan smiled; Carter was not going to defeat Fujiwara. The missiles would be launched and the Fujiwara forces gone before the jets on the radar could reach the island.

"Too late, Nick," she said softly. "We'll do it, and we'll get away."

Carter had circled with his back to the launching controls, then suddenly he jumped away from Fujiwara and raised his *katana* to smash it down into the keys and dials of the launch controls. Fujiwara leaped in, a reflex move to block Carter's slash at the instrument board.

"Masashige!" Siobhan cried. "No!"

She was too late. Fujiwara, momentarily diverted from Carter himself to the imagined threat to his launch controls, exposed his body and Carter slashed, almost cutting him in half through the leather armor with the razor-sharp *katana*.

"So?" Fujiwara whispered, slowly sinking to the floor as his blood and intestines poured out. "A trick, Killmaster. Only a trick."

"A trick," Carter said. "I couldn't beat you, and I had to beat you."

Fujiwara nodded. "I . . . understand. Your . . . job. I . . . had . . . greater . . . dreams . . . greater . . ."

And Fujiwara was dead.

Carter faced Siobhan.

She looked down at Fujiwara, then at Carter. "It might even have worked, Nick."

"We'll find an easier way."

She nodded, smiled. "Well, I'll make a deal."

"Deal?"

"Who knows, I might even be as good a swordsman as you, still save the day for the bad guys. But I really only wanted Masashige. I'll stop the countdown, and tell you where to find the antidote and neutralizer for the weed. You forget about me." She laughed. "They'll never believe you anyway, and you can't prove it now."

Carter watched her. She went on smiling.

"No deal," he said.

He turned to the console and studied it for a second, then threw six switches and pulled six levers. The dials slowly sank to zero, and the flashing lights of the launch sequence went out. He turned back to Siobhan O'Neill.

"No deal."

She shrugged. "There's still the antidote for the poison and the killer of the seaweed. I'll go quietly, Nick. The politicians will make the deal."

"Let them," Carter said.

He bent, picked up the still bleeding body of Fujiwara Masashige, and carried it out into the corridor and on into the slowly brightening morning sunlight over the vast Pacific. Some of the black-robed soldiers ran up, their guns ready, swords out, and stopped. Carter placed the dead man against the wall of the building, sitting up.

"He's dead," he said in Japanese. "U.S. Navy jets will be here in twenty minutes, maybe less. You can't get away now, and there's nothing more to fight for."

The soldiers stood there looking at their dead leader. Then they dropped their weapons to the ground, turned, and walked away. They would spread the word. It was over. Carter sat down in the morning light beside the body of Fujiwara Masashige.

David Hawk stood on the deck of the carrier and looked back toward the high clouds over the Kwajalein atoll.

"They'll all stand trial in Japan, but I don't expect they'll get much. Loyal to Fujiwara and his crazy ideas, that's all."

"That's enough," Carter said. "Crazy ideas can kill."

"And did," Hawk said. "But thanks to you, Nick,

there's no permanent or long-term damage. Scott will have that base back to normal in a month, and he loved every second of the fighting.''

"Siobhan?''

Hawk scowled, and chewed his cheap cigar. "I said no deal—Canberra should charge her as Fujiwara's partner. We'll come up with the antidote and the weed neutralizer sooner or later. I hope they throw the goddamned book at her!''

"Will they?''

"Of course not. They'll deal, and they'll get what she knows. She'll lie, retire from the service, and probably live on a pension from ten governments.''

"Yeah,'' Carter said. "What about Sam and his Kwajaleinis? They want their island back.''

"Talk to Congress, Nick. When you get back from your next job, that is.''

Carter walked away. He wanted some cold sea wind on his face. Maybe Fujiwara Masashige hadn't been so very crazy after all. Maybe not crazy at all.

DON'T MISS THE NEXT NEW
NICK CARTER SPY THRILLER

TERROR TIMES TWO

Carter parked the nondescript staff Opel two blocks away and killed the engine. He lit a cigarette, surveyed the street and then the hotel.

Even with a chill breeze from the ocean and the continuing drizzle, there were a few night people out: streetwalkers, pimps, drunk seamen, and grifters looking for an easy mark.

The Hotel Penguin was a mess.

Strictly speaking, the hotel part was used mostly as a flophouse by itinerant merchantmen and the denizens of the downstairs bar and the street on an hourly basis.

The bar had a very limited clientele, all bad.

The brick facade and entry were crumbling and badly in need of paint. The whole building looked like a decayed tooth. Most of the people strolling in and out of the bar had the same appearance.

That was why Carter had chosen it. He, in a single-breasted blue suit over a white turtleneck, would stand out like the proverbial sore thumb. Vandrostov and any of his team, even if they donned the attire and the grime, would do the same.

The four employees of the Hungarian restaurant Gretchen Mochner had contacted had spread like the four winds. It had been impossible to nail each of them, but Haynes's people were pretty sure that some kind of contact had been made to their control.

The Killmaster could only hope word had drifted upward to Vandrostov. Of course, even if it had, there was no guarantee the boss man would show up to do his own dirty work. In fact it was more than likely he wouldn't. He would probably send two or three underlings, and hope Carter could be taken out without any risk to himself or his current assignment.

And that brought up other questions. Was Vandrostov's presence in Lisbon directly related to Maria Ketis and her friend? Or was that and the "Alex" story merely a smoke screen?

The Killmaster had no real hope of nailing the wily Russian master spy and executioner this night. The whole show was to take prisoners. If they got one of the man's team, Haynes's people were equally as adept and ruthless as the Russians in the matter of making someone talk.

Hopefully, that talk would give them a trail to Vandrostov himself.

Carter took a last look-see at the street and its buildings. Rob Haynes and his people were there somewhere, but he couldn't spot them.

Which was as it should be.

He stepped from the car and locked it. Between car and bar he was hit by a couple of panhandlers and scrutinized by each of the hookers. He could tell by the way they looked away that they had sized him as a cop, or a man who was looking for something besides an hour or so of fun.

The bar was crowded, tight skirts and tighter sweaters on the women, pea jackets and turtlenecks on the men. They made him from the door to the window, and then dismissed him.

He ordered a beer, no glass, and when it came, he settled back to wait. A couple of the girls made propositions with their eyes; another one, in a raincoat, walked directly up to him. Smiling, she opened the coat.

She had nothing on underneath it.

Carter smiled and shook his head.

"Police?"

"Tourist."

"Then why don't you want woman?"

"I've got a disease."

She shrugged and moved on.

Halfway through a second beer, a fight broke out between two drunks near the bar. Neither of them could land a punch, so no one seemed very interested. But when one of them tripped over his own feet and crushed a chair on his way down, the bartender stepped in. One swing for each from a rock-hard fist, and both of them were deposited in the rear alley to cool off.

Through it all, Carter cased the men in the bar one by one. Years of well-honed instinct told him that it was a lost cause. Not a single man would fit the bill of one of Vandrostov's bullyboys.

At nine o'clock he gave it up and paid his bill at the bar.

That's when he got the surprise.

"You American?" asked the beefy bartender, not bothering to offer any change from the bill.

"Yeah."

"Carter?"

"Yeah."

The big man passed across a grimy envelope and moved away before Carter could ask about the source.

Inside was a brief, typed note. He read it on the way to the door:

My dear Nicholas: Are you mad, or just naïve? The Mochner woman is a nymphomaniacal, romantic idiot. I would take any report from her as worthless. However, if you do show up and receive this, treat it as a warning. Stay out of my hair on this one. What is done is done and cannot be undone. Regards, V.

Carter chuckled and stuffed the note into his pocket. The man was right, of course. It had been a rather simple ploy, but one that had to be done nevertheless.

Outside, he dropped his cigarette to the pavement and ground it under his left heel.

It was a signal. Right, they are on me. Left, no game, go home.

The car's engine purred to life. He drove to the dead end of the block where the seawall made a large half circle, and made a U-turn.

He was about fifty feet on his return when an old truck charged out of a narrow alley. The truck caught the Opel full on the right front fender. The little car spun around and went up on two wheels.

Carter held his breath and, at the same time, cursed his carelessness. The note had been a nice touch, put him off guard, made him look at himself as foolish for even thinking that Vandrostov would take the bait.

Finally, the car came down on all four wheels and the Killmaster slid out the door.

They were coming from both sides. From the footsteps, he guessed three. There was no time for Wilhelmina, or even Hugo. They were on him like blitzing linemen on a fallen quarterback.

Trying to come up, he took a knee in his side and a well-aimed boot in his thigh that numbed his whole right leg.

Before the kicker could get in a second one, Carter rolled, knocking the man's legs from beneath him. He started down with a grunt, and ended up with a howl when Carter brought the heel of his hand up into his nose.

The Killmaster continued his roll and managed to come up on one knee as the other two came on for the kill. The one to his left came in low, like a wrestler, with only his hands. The other, to Carter's right, had two feet of pipe in his hand.

Carter chose to get rid of the pipe first.

When the man swung, Carter ducked under the pipe. He got the forearm with his left hand, and when the velocity of the swing abated, he grasped the end of the pipe with his right.

As Carter had guessed, the guy was a terrier. Even though the Killmaster held the pipe, so did the terrier.

Carter merely brought it back up and smashed it into the man's grinning face. Teeth splintered, and a spitting howl of pain sent blood spurting from the man's splayed lips.

But the heavyweight on the left had kept coming.

Carter felt a blow in the belly, another just above the left knee. It was like being kicked by a horse.

He coughed, felt himself go down to his left knee, and desperately jabbed four fingers into the man's throat. The eyes went wide and gleamed white around the dark pupils.

But he was far from done.

A heavy arm came down over the Killmaster's neck like a poleax.

The street blurred and swam before his eyes.

Still gagging, his mouth opening and closing like a fish out of water, the killer bent forward. His arms flailed until his hamlike hands found Carter's throat.

Carter made a half fist, knuckles bent, and stabbed again. He saw the other man's eyes roll up, and the pressure on his throat released.

He rolled away the dead weight, only to find numbers one and two rejoining the fray. One of them had a long, ugly knife.

Enough was enough.

Carter unleathered Wilhelmina and brought her barrel up under the chin of the one he had already mangled with the pipe. The blow had barely roared out of the barrel when he dealt another dead center in the forehead.

Carter staggered around just as the one with the knife made his lunge. He brought up Wilhelmina but didn't have to fire.

From his right side, Rob Haynes appeared. He moved

around Carter like a striking snake.

"I got him."

"Be my guest," Carter moaned, and backed away.

Haynes wasn't a big man, but he was as fast as lightning.

In one swift motion he had disarmed the man, broken his collarbone, and dislocated his shoulder. The knifer went down like a log, his shirt ripped open. He was screaming in agony as blood spurted past an exposed fragment of his collarbone.

Haynes turned to face Carter, the stub of a cigar still lit in the side of his mouth. "You all right?"

"I'll live," Carter replied.

> —From TERROR TIMES TWO
> A new Nick Carter spy thriller
> From Charter in August 1986